SHADES OF CRUELTY

SARAH URQUHART

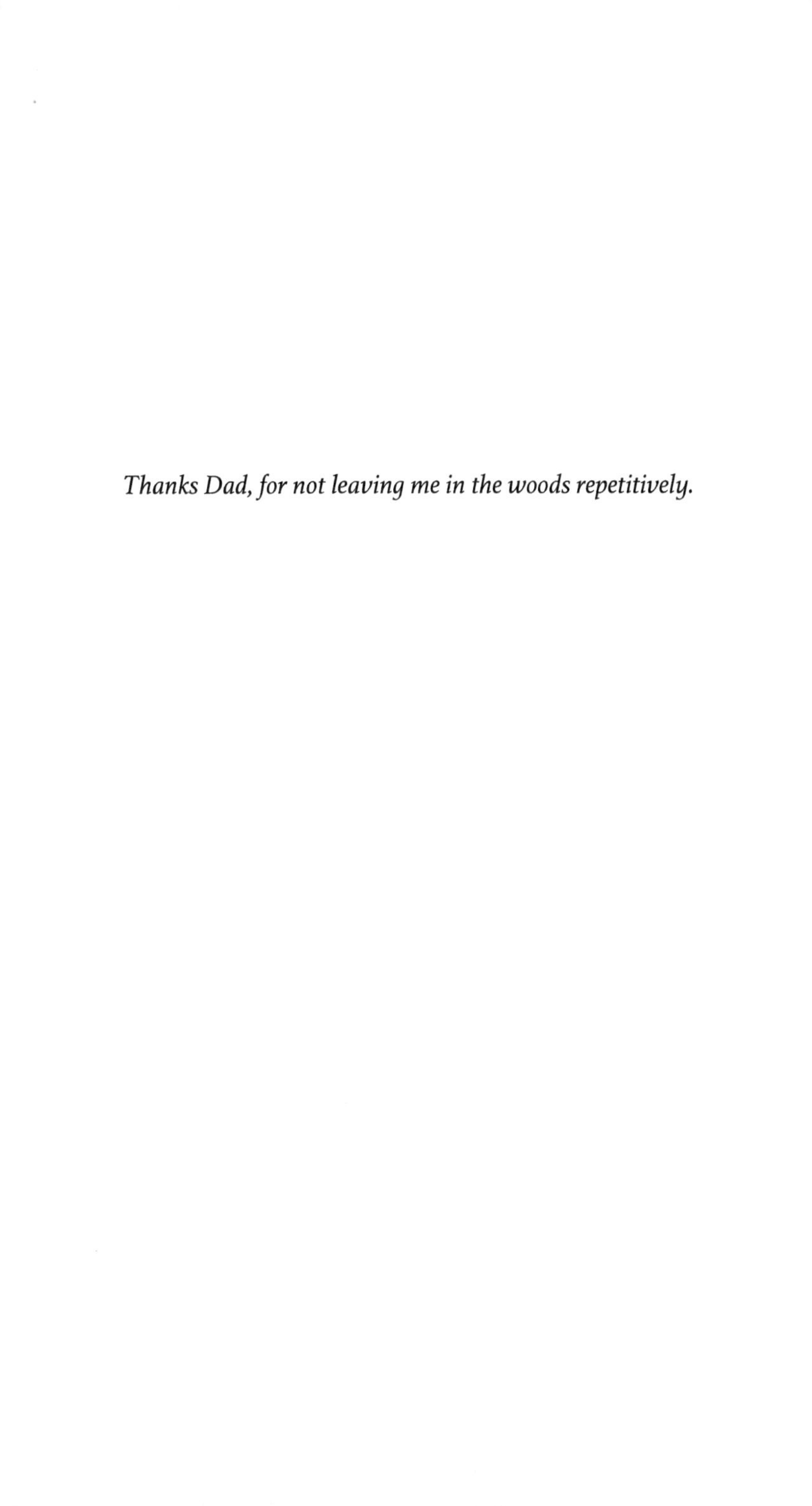

Thanks Dad, for not leaving me in the woods repetitively.

1

The perimeter alarm blared. Its sudden cut off into silence didn't lessen the urgency in the night. King's eyes snapped open, adjusting to the darkness. The familiar shapes and shadows of his bedroom formed in his vision while he waited, keeping perfectly still. When the alarm sounded a second time, he leapt out of bed and paced to his office across the hall. Light from the monitors filled the small room, revealing tail lights disappearing in the dust.

A prickle crawled along the back of his neck and shoulders, an instinct he recognized coming to life. His alarm sounded a third time, but no movement showed on the screen.

He grabbed a pair of sweats and a T-shirt and dressed while on his way to the door. His nature hadn't changed. He'd built the same necessary precautions into his secluded home and security system. If he found something out there, he'd call Dak.

King hiked through the trees adjacent to the half a kilometer long gravel lane leading to his house. His muscles warmed up with the steady and silent walk.

Complete darkness encased the area, the moon and stars hidden behind clouds. But King was used to the night. Old habits helped his eyes adjust, especially to the familiar terrain of his own property. His hike was methodical, watching and listening to everything in the surrounding woods. Whatever crossed his perimeter hadn't been there long and hadn't moved, but it continued to trigger his alarm.

Once deeper into the woods, he approached the end of the lane from the side. Something large lay still about five feet inside the trees of his property. *Fuck.* Annoyance made his jaw lock and he let out a tight breath. Seemed someone decided to use his property as a dumping ground. That large lump resembled a body. How ignorant could someone be to leave a body on private property?

The mass moved and let out a faint moan. King stood still and frowned, waiting to see if they were conscious. The body lay still once again, and he approached, kneeling down to turn them onto their back.

Air stalled in his throat at the unexpected sight of a pale, feminine face. He felt for her pulse and did a quick check for injuries.

Leaving her here wasn't an option. Inwardly sighing, King hooked one arm around her shoulders and another under her knees. Taking the lane instead of the woods, he carried her back to the house. She'd been limp until about halfway there. A soft moan, a low tone of discomfort, came from her throat. Each of her muscles tensed as her body turned toward him. Her eyes swayed behind her closed lids. King froze, waiting to see if she'd wake. The skin around her eyes crinkled for only a moment until she sighed, relaxing into him. Her body no longer lay limp against him, but the tenseness disappeared.

The twitch along King's spine heated. That twitch had

saved his life hundreds of times. It could be someone choosing random land for dumping. But he trusted his instincts more than assumptions.

This woman was no good.

After reaching his house and maneuvering his way in the door, he laid her down on his couch. Retrieving his phone from his room, he dialed Dak on his way back.

"Dak." An alert but groggy baritone echoed over the line. King's eyes roamed over the girl. Long, black, wavy hair spread over the arm of the couch and her shoulders.

"This is Dak." Dak snapped, breaking King's concentration.

"Need you at my place."

"Got it." The call ended. King expected Dak within the hour. He itched to review his security footage, but he didn't want to leave the girl unsupervised.

King had left that world, having amassed enough darkness in his almost forty years. He didn't want trouble on his doorstep. He didn't want to go back to that life. The life of death deals and deceit. King had escaped with no one knowing his face. Getting out while his identity was still intact had been necessary.

The twitch in his back increased, pinching its way up and down. This girl would bring trouble, if she wasn't trouble herself. And King didn't want to have anything to do with it.

EMBER BELLAMY WOKE, but her eyes wouldn't open. Her lids--heavy and weighted--stuck as if clumped with too much mascara after a night out. She tried to move her arms and her skin clung to the surface beneath her. Smooth, stiff fabric. Ember froze. Her father didn't own leather furniture. Fear slithered through her. She wasn't where she should be. Events from the night before played in her head. Nothing had happened. Nothing out of the ordinary. Ember had made dinner for her and her father. He'd spent the evening in his office while Ember had watched a movie before going to bed early in her childhood bedroom.

Ember kept her breathing even and listened. Goosebumps peppered her exposed arms and legs, and her skin tightened from the cooler air.

As she cracked open her eyes, pain lanced through her head. Squeezing them shut, she took a breath. With her next attempt, she squinted while her vision adjusted. Piercing pain spiked in her head like one of her worst hangovers, not that she had many to compare to. But Ember didn't drink when she visited her father.

A lamp on an end table at her feet gave the room a low glow. She was in a living room, not her father's.

Ember searched the room for any clues or a way out. A strangled scream caught in her throat when she laid eyes on a man standing in the shadows several feet away. She tried to sit herself up and move herself further into the couch. Weak, heavy muscles made her movements clumsy. Her limbs needed time to regain strength.

The man didn't move when she choked on her own scream or when she flopped around on the couch. He stood in shadows thanks to the dim light. It seemed like a purposeful move. Unable to see his face, Ember imagined it as stiff as the rest of his body. Tall, broad, thick arms crossed over his bare chest. They stared at each other for long moments.

"Who are you?" The hoarse sound scraped along her dry throat.

"You first." Those two words seemed to deepen the darkness. Despite being afraid, she frowned in confusion.

"Ember Bellamy." She whispered to help her throat adjust. His head cocked to the side, allowing the light to hit the line of his jaw. With no response from him, she imagined he expected her to say more. But she only repeated her question.

"Who are you? Where am I?" She hesitated. "Did you kidnap me?" She was making her way into a sitting position, but she moved without taking her eyes off him.

"It doesn't matter who I am." His pause weighted the silence. "And I didn't kidnap you."

Ember had sat herself up on the couch by now. "Then how did I get here?" Her fear grew. Maybe he had someone else take her and bring her to him.

"I'd like to know the answer to that same question." His voice resonated with threat. "Why don't we start with why someone would want to kidnap you?"

"How would I know?" She snapped the words at him and he took a quick step toward her, bringing himself closer to the light. She flinched and amended, more calmly, "I don't know." But now that he stood in the light, his face didn't look like a friendly one. Ember imagined the ridiculously handsome features of a thirty-something man morphing into whatever he needed, from charm to pure evil. But right now, the rigid jaw line and dark eyes held a purpose--to frighten her. It worked.

A breeze ruffled the hair on the back of her head. Ember wanted to turn around, but she refused to take her eyes off the threat in front of her. She jumped at the sudden appearance of another man walking past her on silent feet.

"Someone left me a package, but I don't know who or why and apparently neither does she." Both sets of eyes turned to her as they continued their conversation. Her body shivered and not from the cold. Ember swallowed and bit her cheek to keep from making a sound under their scrutiny.

"Security catch anything?" The voice was low, rough with damage. With the silence and stillness of the night, she felt the vibrations.

"I only saw the car speeding off. I've been busy since then." Staring at her. The newcomer left, walking down a hall on the other side of the room.

With her adrenaline gone, she shivered. Way too much of her was on display for this man. She didn't want to see where his eyes wandered.

He moved, his massive figure making waves in the room. Ember startled.

"Don't move."

She swallowed and didn't think to disobey him. He left down the hall and returned with a blanket. Throwing it through the air, it landed in a misshapen ball on her bent knees. Ember unfolded it and scrambled to cover herself up to her chin.

She mumbled out a thank you, uncertain what to make of the small act of kindness. "Can I at least know who you are?"

"No." An immediate and direct answer.

"Or where I am?"

"My home," he growled, territorial and threatening. Ember hoped the blanket hid the shiver his tone incited. But she doubted he missed anything with the way he watched her, studied her.

"I'm sorry." Ember looked down at where her knees hid beneath the wool. With him just as confused, she voiced the unnecessary apology as a last resort.

"For what?"

"I'm sorry for whatever this is. I really don't know anything. I went to sleep in my own bed last night and woke up here. So please, if you're lying and you did kidnap me and bring me here, tell me, but if not, I'm sorry. I just want to go home." Ember wanted to forget the whole thing. Leave and move on. He hadn't hurt her. She could let this go.

A deep sound from the back of his throat pushed out a hard and heavy sigh. Ember didn't want to look. She didn't want to see that he'd lied and everything was about to turn more frightening.

"Where's home?" If he had kidnapped her, he wouldn't need to ask. Ember rattled off her father's address, adding the city as well. The night's twister may not have left her in proverbial Kansas.

"That's my father's house. I'm staying with him for the summer." Maybe it hadn't been wise to give that much information. But it was too late now. She just wanted to figure out what happened from there. Not here with a brooding mountain of a man judging her.

When he said nothing else, Ember tightened her fingers on the blanket and pulled it tighter--like a shield as she looked back up at him.

"His name." Not a question, only a clear demand for information. He'd been waiting to meet her gaze.

"Samuel Bellamy," Ember answered. His almost black eyes never left her face while he seemed to think through everything she said.

"Come with me." He walked away, but turned when she didn't follow. Ember peeled the blanket back and put her feet on the floor. She hadn't expected the effort it took to push her weak body to stand. Each part of her dragged as if in a deep sleep. She pulled the blanket around her shoulders and held it together in front of her. He didn't continue until she had taken several steps toward him.

He walked down the same hall the other man had and opened a door, but didn't go in. His broad frame blocked the opening so Ember couldn't see inside.

"Find anything?"

"Nothing. What do you want to do?" She heard the gravely timber from inside the room.

"I'm taking her home. You stay here." He didn't wait for a response, just shut the door and turned to face her.

"You're going to take me home?" The incredulous words slipped past her lips as she tilted her head back. And back. His entire frame engulfed her, and his face hardened. No answer came. Ember clutched at the blanket, sure her knuckles were white beneath it. She took a step back to escape his presence, but he gripped her arm to push her in front of him. She had no choice but to trust the man that might have kidnapped her.

KING STEERED Ember out of the house, forcing her to walk ahead of him. He read the surprise in Dak's eyes and his still shoulders. But without information to go on, King had no reason not to assume Ember was innocent. He might be a master of evil, but he wouldn't hurt the girl if she didn't deserve it. Taking her home could be a mistake. King was willing to take the risk. For now.

"You're really taking me home?" Her steps faltered sideways when she turned her head over her shoulder. King lifted an arm and pointed to the front door on the other side of the living room. Her steps slowed outside as she maneuvered over the gravel.

Maybe it was the late hour and being woken up, but his patience vanished. King stepped up beside her. Bending, he scooped her up and stalked to the car. Setting her down, he opened the passenger door. Ember stood with shocked eyes rather than getting into the car.

"In."

She turned herself around and lifted the blanket out from under her as she climbed in. The thump of the shutting door started King's count to five. Ember hit all his hot buttons, but she was the start of something. Something that had disturbed his two years of peaceful retirement.

Once in the driver's seat, he turned to her before starting the car. A threat was best delivered with direct eye contact. "Use the blanket to cover your eyes. Don't drop it until I say. If I catch you looking, I'll blindfold you with your own shirt."

Her breathing stalled, and she pulled the blanket up over her head, holding it together in front of her face. King waited a moment before starting the car. Seemingly innocent bystanders stuck in the middle of this world weren't usually true innocent bystanders. But he followed more than experience.

He pulled away from the house, keeping watch on the trees ahead and behind through the rear-view mirror. Dak would have done the same coming in. As he looked to the right, he saw the blanket move. The rest of her sat stiffly beneath it. Tips of fingers held open a crack in the front.

King shook his head. He couldn't have her lead anyone back to his house. King didn't make idle threats.

Making a sharp turn to the shoulder, throwing her toward the middle of the car, he put the car in park and tore the blanket off her head. She screamed and flailed her arms outward toward him. Struggling, she pushed herself against the door. But it wasn't enough to ward him off. He manacled her wrists into one hand.

"No. Please, don't. I won't look again. I promise."

"Too late, little girl." He pulled her forward and reached for the hem of her top at her back. Yanking it up, he twisted until it tightened in place and he tied a knot. The shirt covered the top half of her face and trapped her arms against her ears.

"You sick bastard." She struggled, attempting to twist her arms free. The blanket sat loosely around her waist and her breasts bounced with her movement. He let her struggle before pulling back onto the road. If he were the sick bastard she claimed, he'd turn on the air conditioning and watch her dusty rose nipples peak.

"You won't like what I do next if you keep struggling or I catch you looking again."

Each of her muscles froze one by one. Her chest only moved with the tiniest of breaths. His lips twitched, but he didn't let loose the grin or chuckle. He enjoyed frightening the girl. Barely audible curses passed her lips and the tank top dampened with tears.

King ignored her and concentrated on watching for signs of being followed. This wasn't his doing, and he was trying to make sure this didn't become his problem.

Once closer to the address she gave him, he reached over with one hand and released the knot in her shirt. Ember pulled the warped shirt back into place. Lifting the blanket, she tucked it around her shoulders and slumped back against the seat.

He pulled to the curb several houses from her father's and on the opposite side of the street. The clock in the car read just shy of two in the morning and the streets had been quiet as soon as they entered the suburban areas. Despite not being followed, King wouldn't risk being seen dropping her off in front of her father's house.

"I can't take you closer." He turned toward her. Reddened eyes matched her flushed face.

"Thank you for bringing me home." Grudging humbleness slowed her words. Not a bit of it sincere. Peeling the blanket from her shoulders, she fidgeted with it in her lap. Uncertainty plagued her frown. Most likely over why he brought her home. He didn't want the trouble of whatever someone tried to throw at him.

"Be careful." He nodded to the door, indicating she get out. He should have sent her off with a better warning than just a lowered tone. But he couldn't, not when she could be an innocent pawn. He'd been rough enough.

King watched her walk down the sidewalk on her tiptoes, avoiding small rocks or debris. She crossed the road the same way when she reached her father's house. Trying the door, it didn't move. Reaching along the side of the door frame, she produced a key and went inside. Ember paused, one hand on the frame and the other holding the door, but didn't look back. A moment more and she disappeared inside. He waited for ten minutes to see if anything stirred in the neighborhood, then started the car and drove home.

"Well?" Dak asked when King walked through the front door. He sat in the corner chair in darkness. King wouldn't have the chair if Dak hadn't claimed the dark corner as his own.

"Damned if I know what the hell is going on. You?"

"He was covered from head to toe in black. I watched him pull the girl from the back, lay her down in the woods, then speed off. No plates and there's a thousand of those cars around."

"Great." Sarcasm laced his voice. "I'm going back to bed. You should crash in one of the other rooms."

"Already planned on it."

King left Dak to brood alone in his corner and went back to bed. It would be too easy if this was over by simply driving the lost girl home.

2

E mber paused, both hands anchored on the door. Shutting her eyes quelled the urge to look over her shoulder. He couldn't be the one to kidnap her just to return her home that same night after accusing her of--well, she didn't know what he accused her of.

Ember released the tense encounter with a concealed sigh and closed the door. Movement in the sitting room to the left caught her attention. Her father stood, holding a glass of his usual scotch.

"Ember?" His aged face looked at her with a frown.

"Dad." She ran to him, wrapping her arms around his slimming waist. For a moment, she felt like a little girl, clinging to her hero. He fixed all her problems. Slowly raising his arm, he pulled her against him and squeezed.

"What's going on, Ember? Where did you go dressed like that and with no shoes?" He grabbed her shoulder and pulled away, taking his time to look at her appearance. Skipping out in the middle of the night hadn't been something she'd even done in her teen years.

"I was kidnapped, I think." She winced at her own explanation. "I don't know why or who or when or how."

"Slow down." His face turned fierce. "What are you talking about? Kidnapped?"

"I don't know. I wish I did." Fresh tears escaped and trailed down her cheek. Ember swiped at them with the back of her hand. All her fear and embarrassment rushed back, overwhelming her with uncertainty. She felt foolish not having an explanation of what happened.

"How did you get home?"

Ember sucked in a breath, ready to blurt out every detail, but the air stuck. She had no details to give. No location, no name. And telling everything seemed like a betrayal of sorts. Ember owed him nothing. Sure, he brought her home. But *nice* wasn't one of his qualities. A *nice* man wouldn't have done what he did to her in the car. Her cheeks heated at the thought, realizing what he would have seen. He'd stripped her. Humiliation flared alongside the anger under her skin. He'd manhandled her, and with ease. It didn't matter she'd tried to peek. Why wouldn't she?

Ember tamped it all down, blocking the imagine of him looking at her naked chest. Her father stepped back the longer she took to answer. She kept her explanation basic.

"A man found me and brought me home."

"Where did he find you?"

"I don't know. I didn't recognize the area." A partial white lie for her father's sake.

"Could you find your way back there from here?" He gripped her shoulder to make sure she faced him.

"No. It's too dark out." More like all she'd seen was the short distance from his house to the car.

Her father leaned down and kissed her head. "I'm glad

you're safe." He whispered the words against her hair. "We'll stay close to home tomorrow."

"Shouldn't we call the police?"

"You don't know where you were. Do you know who it was that found you?"

She shook her head.

"You're home, Ember. You're safe." His face relaxed for a moment before his lips pursed and his brows turned down and into one. "There's nothing to report."

She guessed he was right. Even if she told her father everything, she didn't have any details, names, or a location. And those would be of the man who found her and brought her home, not the person who took her. Other than waking up in the middle of the night in a strange place, she couldn't even be sure someone had kidnapped her.

"All right." She stepped back. "I'm going back to bed."

"Goodnight, Ember." Her father moved closer and hugged her. "I'm so glad you're safe." She relaxed from the love of her father. It had only been the two of them for so long. Her mother had been gone since she was just a little girl. She remembered little and her father didn't speak of Ember's mother. Anytime she asked what happened, her father shut down.

"Goodnight, Dad." Ember climbed the stairs to her room. Stopping in the doorway, she looked to see what the kidnapper had disturbed. Nothing. Her room was just as she'd left it. The bedding was folded back as if she'd risen from bed on her own. Her father hadn't known she was missing. Nothing in the house looked disturbed. Moving to her bedroom window, she checked the lock and inspected the edge. Still nothing.

Ember sighed. Changing her pajamas, she went back to bed, curling into sheets that didn't feel right. She considered showering, not knowing what she'd been through tonight, but decided sleep was a higher priority.

Running through the events had her second guessing what happened. Images of *him* danced through her mind. He'd been a terrifying sight to wake up to, but not once had he been rough, physically. Even when blindfolding and tying her, his firm hands hadn't hurt or left a mark. It would be a deadly mistake to believe he couldn't or wouldn't hurt her. A dark soul shone through his eyes.

Ember fell asleep, puzzled and confused, dreaming of darkness.

HOURS SPENT SCOURING the security footage left them with nothing more than the average size of the man and the make and model of the car. They'd put time into a background check on Samuel Bellamy. A successful lawyer. Lost his wife over twenty years ago. He'd been an only child who'd followed in his father's footsteps. Nothing had alerted any red flags to make them search deeper. There was no connection between Samuel Bellamy and King.

Instead of continuing to waste time, King had sent Dak home by midday.

Instincts screamed at King that this wasn't over, keeping him awake until after midnight. He heard the perimeter alarm on the first sound. King's feet hit the floor a second later. In his office, the monitors showed a man covered in black pulling a female form from the back seat of the same car.

"Fuck." Grabbing pants and his phone, he ran out the door. He waited for Dak to answer, but cut him off. "She's back." Shoving his phone in his pocket, he ran up the lane rather than hiking quietly through his property. King reached the end of the lane in time to see the dissipating dust and hear the engine in the distance.

Holding in his curse, he turned to the female form left behind. She looked frail and vulnerable on her side with the forest debris disturbed around her. And vulnerable she was. He could do anything to her. There were certain expectations attached to his name. No one would expect this woman to survive, or at least leave his presence unharmed.

But her soft features in sleep and the black veil of hair implied innocence. He couldn't ignore this, or make the mistake of letting his guard down with Ember. Even the most dangerous people in the world made themselves appear harmless. He was one of them.

King lifted her and returned to the house. Once again, she wore pajamas, but instead of shorts, she wore pants. The tank top clung to her figure, outlining her breasts he'd memorized the night before.

He laid her on the couch and left her to watch the footage. Sitting down, he started the recording. An almost identical video as the previous night played on the screen. A man dressed in black pulled Ember from the car and deposited her on the ground, but this time, he paused before leaving her. When King showed up on the screen, he shut it off and left to watch over Ember until Dak arrived. He sat in Dak's corner chair so she wouldn't see him when she woke.

She stirred and shivered as the night breeze blew in from the door. Dak glanced at Ember.

"What do you plan to do?"

"I don't know. Not much we can do without knowing what's going on." He needed to see Ember's reaction.

"I'll keep digging." Dak's mind and hands never stopped.

The two of them had worked well together, balancing each other when needed. Dak may not have retired, but the world didn't know he existed.

But King was a wanted man, even in retirement. They craved the identity that followed the name, the title he'd earned. Despite coming face to face with the king of mercenaries, most didn't know who he was.

Blackened and burned on the inside, King believed he'd needed to retire.

A groan from the couch refocused his thoughts.

"What the hell?" Ember's groggy curse accented the sweet huskiness of her voice. The purr shot straight to his cock. His own amusement and arousal just pissed him off. Only two years of retirement and he turned soft toward a sweet-looking girl.

Reminding himself of who he was, King waited for her to fully wake.

Whatever drugs they'd used on Ember caused her slow movements as she lifted her hand to her head. She swayed until she had enough control to pull her knees up to her chest. The soft light showed off her pale face. Dreary eyes searched the room. Sighing, she rested her cheek on her knees with her face toward him. She gasped and squeezed her legs tighter when she caught his gaze through the shadows.

"What the hell, indeed. Let's try this again. Why are you here?" Deepening his voice, it carried across the room without effort.

"I don't know." Panic lanced each word. Part of this or not, the kidnapper had drugged and left her behind. A panic attack was the last thing King wanted to deal with. He stood and moved to a chair closer to the couch. He leaned back with his hands lazing on the arms and an ankle over the opposite knee.

"What happened after I took you home?"

"My father was awake. He asked where I'd been. I told him what happened, and I went to bed." She moved her head up and down as if ticking off events.

"What exactly did you tell him?" His tone filled in the words *every single detail.*

"I said I had been kidnapped and that a man found me and brought me home." Although she still quaked with panic, her voice gained strength as she focused.

"That's it?" He found it odd that's all she would say.

"It's not as if I could have said who you were or where I am. I don't know either of those. And I have no idea what happened between going to sleep in my bed and waking up here." She looked at him accusingly. She had a point, and he wouldn't apologize or offer information now.

"And what about during the day?" King kept the frown off his face and out of his tone. Did her father do nothing?

"My dad worked from home except for a couple of meetings he couldn't reschedule and he told me not to leave the house. That's it."

King eyed her until she squirmed. Holding in a sigh and a need to run his hand over his face, he stood. "Come with me."

She'd had plenty of time for her strength to return to carry her own weight. When she stood and seemed steady, he led her down the hall. King didn't understand why he'd built a house with four bedrooms, but right now they were about to come in handy. Especially since he'd had the forethought to put the locks on outside of two of the rooms.

Stopping at the farthest one down the hall, he opened the door. "Wait in there."

Ember peeked in the room, then stepped away from both him and the door. "Why?"

"In." His threat whipped--either get in the room or he'd put her there. She visibly swallowed, the movement down her smooth throat catching his attention with unwelcome arousal. Ember walked into the room without turning her back on him. She had some sense of self preservation.

Once Ember cleared the door, King closed it and flipped the lock.

"What are you doing? Let me out!" Ember banged against the door. "Let me out of here. I swear, I don't know what's going on."

King waited until her protests died and the sound of her sliding against the door to the floor created silence. He stepped into the office to check on Dak.

"He paused." Dak stared at a screen showing the man standing over Ember. "He paused before leaving her. It's someone she knows." Dak spun the chair around and crossed his arms over his chest. "Still think she's innocent?" A slight hitch in Dak's face challenged King.

"Yes." Every single thing he'd learned since a young teen said Ember had to be part of this, that he should deal with the threat accordingly. But he couldn't lie to himself. "Innocent or not, I've locked her in the spare bedroom for now."

"King. It's likely she's in on it."

"But what is *it*?" King's frustration slipped. "Why kidnap someone to drop her off on someone's doorstep who didn't ask for her?"

"To frame you." The calm reply dropped in the room, heavy with the implications it carried, with the threat of holding a bright red target.

"We need to find out who that man is. And how he knows who I am." King pointed to the paused screen. "We'll take her home again tomorrow night, but you'll stay to watch."

King stalked to his room, passing the muffled sobs coming from Ember. He shut his door, blocking out the sound. Her feelings weren't his problem.

<hr>

AFTER CRYING AT THE DOOR, Ember wiped the wetness from her face. Her hands shook with fury. It wouldn't do her any good. She was helpless against any of this. Helpless against who took her and helpless against the man that locked her in here. Assuming they weren't the same person. Her fear and anger rose on a red hot spike up her spine.

Ember tried the window, deciding the black night and unknown terrain were a better option than waiting for him to let her out. The lock didn't budge. What the hell was it made of? She searched the room for something to pry it open, but found nothing.

Her fingers rubbed across her forehead as she strode across the room to the large bed. The softness of the covers surprised her. Nothing about that man or his house seemed soft. The room he had left her in was bare of any gentle belongings. But the slate grey bedding sunk low under her weight. Hugging her knees, Ember leaned back against the headboard.

Her head ached as it chiseled on more than one mystery. Who took her and who kept her. She had no reason to believe the man out there hadn't taken her. Except he'd been furious to find her in his territory. Every move, sound, expression he'd made had been to incite terror. But he'd never threatened to hurt her. Oh, it was there, between the lines, in the clench of muscles, the stark snare of his gaze. He could hurt her and would if she gave him reason.

The dark eyes and sharp jawline promised danger. And yet he'd taken her home.

Hours of drifting in and out of an uncomfortable sleep left a cramp in Ember's neck. The pain stretched down one shoulder. She'd resisted the temptation of the comfortable bed, only wanting to be free and home. The door swung open, flying fear toward her. She jumped to her feet and winced as her muscles spasmed.

He lounged against the frame with his arms crossed. Dark, damp hair slouched in disarray on his head, strands reaching toward his eyes. The small room filled with the scent of a woodsy, male fragrance. A plain T-shirt and jeans replace the low-lying sweatpants of the night before.

"Where did you go?" The question escaped before Ember could think it through.

"I went back to bed." He tilted his head to the side and looked down her body. Ember straightened her pajamas that were already straight.

"You're kidding me." Her anger flushed, the heat creating an itch under her skin. Someone wanted her gone. Maybe the man standing in front of her, and yet she challenged him.

His eyes narrowed, striking her with a reminder of her position, but soon a single brow lifted. "Hungry?" He pushed off the wall and left, leaving the door open for her to follow. She stalled for a moment, as if shocked by freedom.

The house looked more like a mountain cabin as she walked down the hall. The wood trim had a nutty stain that stood out. Passing several doors, she found herself back in the living room. Sunlight streamed inside, evaporating the eerie atmosphere from the past two nights. Clangs of dishes and cupboards echoed through an arched wall on the left.

She found him in the kitchen cracking eggs into a bowl.

"Are you going to take me home?" she asked.

"Probably. I don't know yet." He never looked up from the bowl.

"What is that supposed to mean?" Ember took a breath as her voice hitched. She needed to remember that she needed his help.

"Well," he paused, cocking his head, "I don't know yet." He beat the eggs and added milk. Ember swallowed past the lump in her throat.

The kitchen was dark and oddly cozy, flowing with the rest of the house. Stainless steel appliances, dark cabinets, and marble counters called to her to create a delicious mess with all the things she could make in the massive space.

"You might as well get comfortable. If I take you home again, it won't be until the early hours of the morning."

"If?"

"Yes, if."

Being difficult wouldn't help. Taking a seat at the island, Ember watched him cook. Grating cheese and cutting peppers to add to the bowl. His graceful movements shouldn't surprise her. Muscles flexed as he pushed the knife down over the vegetables. Grace didn't negate his intimidating size.

Frustration welled, but Ember forced it away into its own compartment. She knew nothing of what was happening. If only she knew his name, that would be something.

"What's your name?" Please let him give her this one thing.

"That isn't something you need to know." He glanced over his shoulder, but not to trap her gaze. His eyes moved down to her breasts showing above the counter. Hunching forward, she wrapped her arms over her chest. When this was all over, Ember was going to sleep in sweats for the rest of her life.

"Why? If you didn't kidnap me, then why won't you give me your name?"

Her only answer was the sizzle of the frying pan as he poured the contents from the bowl.

"It's all clean, King." The deep voice from the other night vibrated from her left.

"King?" Ember's voice pitched with excitement. A name. She had a name. Some piece of knowledge. It wasn't anything to get excited over, but she clung onto that information as if it meant her freedom, as if it meant she had control.

King narrowed his eyes at the other man, who shrugged and stuck his hands in his front pockets.

"That's your name?" Ember's stomach dropped as he turned those narrowed eyes on her. Her breath slowed to a stop the longer the silence filled the room. He didn't have to answer her. At least she had something to call him.

King continued to cook. The silence held danger with both of them looming near. The newcomer had lighter colouring in his eyes and hair, but only an idiot would look at him and consider him a gentle giant. Either of them wouldn't fool Ember. She wasn't in the presence of good men.

"Well." King extended the word, turning around with two plates. The scent of the omelettes started a chorus in her stomach. "I guess we'll take you home. But not until tonight."

"Thank you." Her voice softened with genuine gratitude. They weren't the good guys, but they were taking her home.

"You're welcome. Eat." He pushed a plate across the island and they left the kitchen with his own in hand.

Alone, she felt like nothing more than a burden. A problem left for him to solve. But Ember would rather solve her own problems, if people would just let her.

3

———

King turned inside his office once Dak shut the door, ensuring Ember wouldn't overhear. "There's really nothing to find?"

"Nothing. But we've never kept records. Any connection we'd have to remember ourselves."

"Fine." King had to play along. "Take her home tonight and stay to keep watch. Has her father reported her missing?" He forked another bite of the eggs.

"Yes. But details are minimal in the report."

"I expect to find her here again by tomorrow morning."

Dak nodded his agreement before leaving.

King found Ember doing the dishes in the kitchen. He set his plate and fork next to the sink and leaned against the counter beside her. There had to be a connection, but who and why?

Young innocence poured from her. Soft skin, wide eyes. Hell, she was probably more innocent than he suspected. Part of him hoped she was. He'd hate to hurt someone like her. His job may have been evil, but he had standards-- unknown standards that he used at his own discretion. He never hurt the innocent. They didn't deserve that kind of evil touching them and their lives. King didn't drag others into that world unless he had to.

He stood close enough for his heat to encase her, watching her squirm beside him. Once she finished the dishes, Ember faced him, but kept her eyes low.

"You can make yourself at home for the day. As long as you don't leave this house."

"Why don't I just go to the police?" Her eyes looked straight ahead at his chest, and curiosity separated her words. A search for information rather than a threat or accusation. "My father must have reported me missing by now."

"I'm not taking you to the police." They weren't a concern to him, but they wouldn't be of any help. "Besides, I have a suspicion."

"Care to share."

"No, I don't." King suppressed a grin when her huff escaped her pursed lips despite her attempt to hold it back. "Come on. I'll show you where everything is."

King listened to her bare feet across his floor as she followed him from the kitchen and across the living room. "That's a study." He pointed to a large room to the left of the hall. He'd set it up like a library and work space, giving him somewhere to manage the legitimate businesses he'd acquired.

She'd peeked in the open door. Her steps rushed to catch up when he continued down the hall without her.

"Bathroom is here." He tapped on the first door on the right, then continued on to the end of the hall. "You're acquainted with this room. It's yours to use."

"How do you work the locks on the windows?" Effort to hold his gaze shook her shoulders. He didn't know if he should laugh or lock her back in the room. She was going to be a pain in his ass.

King continued on as if she'd never spoken. Stepping back up the hall, he stopped between his room and the security office. Pointing at each of the doors, he pinned her under his glare until she squirmed. "These are off limits." He didn't want to see signs of her in his bedroom, and there was no need for her to know the security he had and why.

"Okay," she whispered, wide eyes lacking the bravado from only seconds earlier.

King finished his tour with a nod and left. He should lock her away, but something else ruled any time he laid eyes on her. She wouldn't find a phone anywhere to call the police or her father and the alarms would sound if she left the house.

Ember followed, her presence easy to pinpoint. King stopped and waited for her to run into him. A brush of air hit his back. Looking over his shoulder, he glared as she caught her balance.

Assuming he'd made his point, he walked into the study, needing to forget the woman invading his space. But Ember stopped in the doorway as he sat behind his desk.

"What do you do?"

He shouldn't answer her, but he considered the question. He was still a deadly man, retirement would never change that. But he spent his days managing his legitimate businesses, traveling, and tending his house and land.

Ember stepped into the room.

"It's better if you don't know." The less she knew, the better. Dak would follow and get whatever information he could and they would deal with the situation.

"Why?" She'd wrapped her arms in front of her, holding

onto her shoulder. A protective gesture to hide herself, yet she'd still followed him to pry answers she didn't need.

"Do you always ask this many questions?"

"It's not like I have anything else to do."

Definitely a pain in his ass. "Read a book." He gestured to the shelves lining the other side of the room, where he hoped she'd stay and leave him alone.

Her sigh released heavily from her nose like a pissed off puppy. King watched her from slitted eyes instead of focusing on the reports from his hotel managers. Sauntering along the wall, she fingered the spines of the books. Sliding one from the shelf, she sat in an armchair closer to him. Her hands clasped the paperback, but she didn't open it, and hadn't looked at it since she pulled it free. Her eyes roamed the room. "Have you read all of these?"

"Yes." If he bought a book, he read it before it landed on his shelf.

Now that Ember had stopped swaying around the room, King forced his focus on the reports. He didn't need to watch her, didn't need to continue to memorize the outline of her curves under the tight top. He didn't need to see every emotion unfolding in her eyes. And Ember didn't need extra encouragement to ask him more questions.

But she did anyway.

"What are you working on?"

He flipped to the next page and ignored her.

"Is King your last name or is it a nickname?"

"Neither," he snapped. Ignoring her proved difficult. With his head still facing down, he cast his eyes upward to look at her.

"Then why did he call you King? Is that your name?" Her eyebrows shot up in excitement, as if she'd found a clue.

Lifting his head up, he pinned her with a heated glare.

"Okay, fine." Her concession only lasted a moment. "Where did you find me?"

"In the woods half a kilometer from here."

"How did you find me? Both times?" Her tone had changed from inquisitive to shaky.

King leaned back in his chair. She'd pulled her legs up onto the chair and, even under her light weight, she sank into the aged leather.

"What? Do you have something else you'd rather talk about?" Challenge filled her eyes, covering up the vulnerability that slipped. She was a brave little pain in the ass.

"I'd rather not talk at all and if you insist on asking more questions, I will find something to gag you with." His own threat incited delicious reels in his mind of Ember bound and gagged in that chair while he finished his work. He wouldn't make the struggle to get her there unpleasant for her.

Ember lifted her fingers to cover her lips. But she struck him with another challenge in her narrowed eyes. He met it, hoping she'd give him a reason to follow through. As soon as his lips twitched, her hand dropped, and so did her eyes.

Disappointing relief turned him back to the waiting papers on his desk.

All his businesses were under different aliases. New ones were always ready in the cue if needed. He'd left his real name behind the day he started walking the streets. He'd had many names over the years. Several had died. But the name King he had earned rather than chosen. He'd kept it for himself and only a select few knew the face matching the name. Living in retirement hadn't changed him.

"I'm scared, King." His name on her wavering lips shocked him out of his concentration. Her eyes said so much--more than he could keep up with. "I don't know why or who would do this. I don't know who to trust and who not to trust. Maybe I shouldn't trust you, but I can't change that."

"You shouldn't trust me."

Ember tilted her head away from the still unopened book.

"I don't have a choice. You didn't take me and you won't hurt me." Her confidence surprised him. It should bother him.

"No. I didn't." But that didn't mean he wouldn't.

Ember nodded and chewed on the inside of her cheek. Pulling in a breath, she straightened her shoulders. "What do you do?" Hesitancy hushed her question, but she looked at him with hope for something. She might as well understand the danger she was in.

"I do bad things and I do them very well." King didn't miss her intake of breath, but he fought not to react under her scrutiny. Her eyes tried to peel away his statement.

"What part of that is a lie?" She saw too much. Instead of scaring her with the truth, she'd only become more inquisitive. An excellent quality for someone so young, except when it involved him.

A lesson she needed to learn.

King stood and walked toward her from around the desk. He trapped her eyes in his, daring her not to look away. Stopping at her knees, he towered over her a moment before blocking her in the chair with a hand on either arm. His shoulders pulled back as he lowered his face to only inches from hers. Her scent invaded his senses, genuine femininity rather than overpowering perfumes and products. Deep breaths pushed her chest upward, giving him a sight to appreciate.

Ember flinched the longer he stayed there, but his

respect for her grew when she didn't shrink back into the chair. Vibrant green eyes broke contact with his to search his face. Hot breath brushed his neck in quicker succession. She hadn't pulled away from him, but his intimidation worked.

Good.

King enjoyed the moment. Enjoyed the emotions rolling off her and the time to study each of them.

Ember had tucked her hair behind her left ear, showing off an upper ear piercing. The stud connected to a silver fili-gree cuff on the shell by a fine chain. Decorative and simple-
-like the woman.

He let his gaze rove her face, down her neck, and over her chest. His intention registered before he answered her question.

"Did. But that doesn't mean I can't or won't." King pulled in her scent one last time. Traces of sweet citrus hit his cock. Damn it. "Be careful what you ask, girl."

THE EFFORT not to react to King strained her lungs. She couldn't hide it all from him, but Ember didn't want to back down. She'd already known he wasn't a good person, but he would have hurt her by now if that had been his intention.

King straightened and strolled back to his desk. Ember allowed her lungs relief with quiet, steady breaths. Despite his warning, she wanted more. But she held back and at least attempted to read to pass the time. As long as she could draw her attention away from King's broad shoulders, stretching the shirt that did nothing to hide his strength to harm.

Ember had to walk a fine line.

Opening the book, she read. The words blurred as they entered her mind, never finding purchase. After the fifth time trying to read the first page, she slapped the cover closed on the book.

"What is it now?" King ground the words low through his teeth. Only his eyes looked up from the desk, irritation glazing over them.

"Are you doing anything to figure out what's going on?" Ember tempered her tone, hoping she didn't give him a reason to make good on his threat to gag her. After the car ride home the other night, she didn't doubt he'd do it.

"Yes." Sharp consonants snapped with his annoyance.

"Is there anything I can do to help?" Helpless and ignorant, she wanted to try.

King straightened the papers on his desk and pushed them to the side. Leaning forward, he eyed her with a focus that worried her. "You can tell me about your father."

"My father?"

He nodded.

"What do you want to know?"

"Work? Hobbies? Friends or associates?"

"He's a lawyer. He may have some friends from the office. And his poker buddies. He's had the same poker friends since I was a kid."

King picked up his phone, his thumb making quick motions over the screen. He placed it to his ear until the ringing stopped. He set it on the desk and put it on speaker. "Their names."

"Why are you asking about my father and his friends?"

"Their names," he repeated slower.

"I don't know if I can remember their last names." Ember listed off four of her father's friends, guessing at a couple surnames. His friends had been around most of her life. She could recite their nicknames in a heartbeat.

"Run those." King ended the call.

"Am I allowed to know his name, the guy you were just talking to? I assume it's the same guy that's been here." She didn't understand all the secrecy. Even a fake name would make her happy. Something more than *that guy, newcomer,* or *not-so-gentle giant.*

"That's up to him." King shrugged.

"Okay. Now what do we do?" This was a start, but she needed to do more.

"Nothing." Instead of going back to his work, he stared at her. Deep eyes saw too much. Ember rubbed the shiver off her arm.

"I can't just sit here."

"Then don't."

Ember sighed. "What do you suggest I do?" Her tempered tone dripped with mock sweetness as she tilted her head.

"You're holding a book." He nodded to the book sitting in her lap.

"It's not enough. I can't focus on it."

"Clearly," he drawled.

"I want to talk or do something physical." Ember slapped the book on the end table beside her, abandoning it entirely.

"I'm not much of a talker."

Ember realized her mistake when a half smile kicked up his lips. His eyes seared when they landed on her breasts. And the damn things perked up under the attention. He wasn't only dangerous, but a predator. And she was the only prey in the room.

"That is not what I meant." She added a bite to her words, hoping to draw his attention back to her eyes. It didn't work. Her body lit up, but she needed to get out of range before it burned. Her skin heated with a rush. King wouldn't be the type of man to miss her reaction. She needed to leave.

Ember fought the urge to squirm. She stood and walked across the room, holding her head up. Heat encased her wrist. King leaned closer.

"Don't leave the house, Ember." His voice held enough warning that if leaving had been her plan, she'd think twice about it now.

"I won't."

He only waited a moment more before tearing his eyes away and nodding, letting go of her wrist. Ember left, unintentionally slamming the door behind her, and walked several feet before placing her hand where King's had been. She closed her eyes and sucked in air. Ember needed to get herself under control. A man like King would tear her apart at the scent of her attraction. But she feared it was already too late.

4

King's concentration left on Ember's heels. He'd struggled to finish what he needed for two hours. That had been plenty of time to leave Ember unsupervised. He wondered if she'd get into any mischief or if she'd behave herself. How big of a pain in the ass was she going to be?

Stopping outside the study, he listened for movement. Soft muttering broken up with the occasional clink of silverware came from the kitchen. Before following the sounds, he retrieved one of his T-shirts from his bedroom. The only thing he'd focused on in his study had been her breasts with piqued nipples staring back at him as he'd held her wrist. If he was going to face her again, he needed her covered.

King peered around the arch to the kitchen. Ember paced back and forth behind the island while stopping to stir something on the stove. String wrapped around her hair on top of her head, exposing her neck and shoulders as the tail swayed across her back. Her lips moved and her hands gestured randomly, lecturing an imaginary foe. Either him or the man who kidnapped her.

When she turned to pace in the other direction, King

entered the room. Ember didn't hear his steps. He stopped at the stove and waited for her to turn on her toes in a quick spin. Bouncing off his chest, she stepped back, trepidation shaking her eyes. Pulling in a breath, she wiped away her reaction. Too easily for his comfort. Red streaks of irritation returned over her cheeks and her nostrils flared.

"What are you cooking?" The scents from the pot filled the kitchen with the smell of herbs and spice.

Ember didn't answer. She continued to pace, stepping around him and pinning him with a glare that he found amusing.

King stepped out of her way and waited.

"If you're not calling the police, then what are you doing?" She slammed fists onto her tiny hips. Her eyes flared and her jaw clenched. King couldn't remember the last time someone questioned him. They most likely weren't still living.

"Waiting." He didn't want her to know Dak would follow her tonight after taking her home. If she was part of this, she didn't need to know. If she wasn't, she could tip someone off to the tail. "You didn't answer my question. What are you cooking?"

"It's just soup." She waved her hand at the stove and rolled her eyes. He had the sudden urge to grip her hair and pull the attitude from her. Instead, he moved into her space. He towered over her, making her seem smaller than she was. Ember's shoulders made the slightest movement as King lifted his hand. He ran a finger around the string in her hair. Wrapping the black silk around his hand, he slid down the length.

"You didn't answer my question either." Her breathy tone caught as she stayed still.

"I did."

"Waiting isn't doing something." Ember stepped from his reach, sighing audibly with the space. "Why can't we go to the police? At least that would be a place to start. Where's the other guy? Is he doing something?" Her voice rose as she assaulted him with question after question.

"That's enough." The low demand, despite being quiet, boomed through the space.

She halted, her body stilling. Her throat worked as she swallowed.

"Sit. And put this on." He held out his T-shirt and pointed at the island. Ember backed away from him and sat, frowning at the shirt. King pulled two bowls from the cupboard and dished up the soup, appreciating the heated aroma wafting toward him. Setting the soup on the island, he took the seat next to her.

"Why give me free rein of the house? For all you know, I've poisoned the soup."

"I don't keep poison in the house and I know you didn't come in with any." He waited for her frown to disappear and the shock to register on her face before he leaned over to speak in her ear. "I was thorough."

Ember gasped and slouched over her bowl rather than sitting with excellent posture, pushing out her chest.

"Enough questions, little girl."

This time, she was smart enough to shut up. She pulled the shirt over her head. But King didn't think he liked the subdued woman sitting next to him. It had been so long since anyone had challenged him that taking it from her gave a little taste of something he didn't know he missed.

She steadily ate, then set the spoon down in the bowl when she finished. "May I have a shower?"

She wouldn't look at him. Staying silent, he waited for her to break. To catch her eyes before answering. He wanted to see what was in them. When her gaze lifted, deep green shone back at him. A light sheen that showed a fear he thought had been missing from her since she first arrived.

But was she scared enough to disobey him? She hadn't yet.

King nodded. Ember left without another word. He understood her frustration. But it would be a mistake if they jumped too soon without knowing what was going on. Patience was a key trait King had to learn long ago. He wouldn't still be standing if he hadn't.

EMBER STEPPED into the steaming water, imagining the tension draining off her body with every droplet. The threats were there, behind the voice, behind the eyes, in his touch. But she knew he wouldn't harm her. Why? Why was she so naïve and sure that dangerous man wouldn't hurt her?

She closed her eyes and put her head under the water, enjoying the heavy thud. The image of King leaning over her in his office flashed behind her closed lids. Deep eyes boring into her. His steel arms caging her in. The way his body moved when he stalked across the room. Ember's wrist heated. She snapped her eyes open, feeling his presence. But when she looked down, her hand gripped her in the same place King had.

Releasing her breath on a groan, Ember shook her head. She had more urgent things to worry about than King. Like all this damn waiting. And what she would do when King took her home tonight.

The steam in the bathroom heated her chest when she stepped from the shower. Grabbing the towel she'd set on the counter, she wrapped it over her hair to rub it dry. Spying her pajamas, Ember considered dressing before leaving, but the bedroom was just down the hall. She could dart that way quick enough. Wrapping the towel around herself, she snatched her clothes and ran straight into King's chest waiting outside the door.

His arm lashed out around her back before she retreated. Too close. Too much. Her breathing stopped, and she pressed her lips together. His hand lifted and pushed her tangled, wet hair away from her face. Tracing his fingers behind her ear, he played with her piercing before making a line down her neck. His arm tensed, pulling her harder against him. Even through the thick towel, she felt his erection press against her stomach. Heat followed his finger over her shoulder and across the tops of her breasts, teasing the top of the towel.

"Breathe, Ember." His voice hummed.

Her chest hurt as the air shook in and out.

"I'm taking care of it. Patience." Then he did what she'd feared he would. He closed the distance and pressed his lips to hers. This kiss would haunt her. He tilted his head, laying claim to her mouth. Running his tongue along her bottom lip, forcing a gasp from her throat. Quivers filled her stomach. Push, pull. She didn't know what to do. But Ember doubted he'd allow her any movement. King controlled this.

Ember caved and relaxed. A burning trail followed his still roaming fingers along her damp skin. Firm lips moved hers until he ended the kiss with a nip.

"Remember, little girl. Patience."

King released her and left, turning back toward the living room and study. Ember's knees weakened. Gripping the door, she fought for air to steady herself. Why would he kiss her? Now, more than just his touch seared her.

Rushing to the bedroom, she shut herself in and sat on the bed. Guess she did have to worry about King. She shouldn't want to know more about the man. But she itched to ask him what bad things he'd done.

He'd said he was handling it. Patience was hard when everyone left her in the dark. Ember hated not knowing. But what choice did she have? For now, she'd keep her patience--and her questions--to herself.

KING GAVE EMBER HER SPACE, but he'd expected her to resurface. Late evening arrived with dusk and she hadn't come in search of food. He looked first in her room before going to the study. About to back out, he paused. Ember had her nose in the book she'd picked earlier. Goosebumps covered her arms as she shivered, but her attention never wavered.

He cleared his throat to get her attention. He hadn't intended to startle her, but her large eyes locked on him. She calmed, but another emotion took hold. Her lips parted and King saw the memory of their kiss cross her softening eyes.

"Come to the living room. Bring the book." He didn't wait for her, but went to the kitchen to make her something to eat. Carrying two bowls, King found her in the chair closest to the low fire he'd started. She set the book upside down on her lap when he approached.

"Did you need me out for a reason?"

"You were cold." He passed her the bowl with the leftover soup and set the salad on the side table.

"Oh. Thank you." Her earlier irritation and impatience

had fled. She ate her soup before setting the salad in her lap and picking up the book.

"You'll be going home in a few hours. Use the spare room to get some sleep before you go."

"I appreciate that. But I don't think I can sleep." She took her dishes to the kitchen and returned to the chair and the book, shutting him out. Her hair fell to the side in black waves as she tucked her feet to her ass and sunk into the chair. Her eyes darted back and forth over the pages.

Knowing he'd see her again in the morning, King left. His eyes crossed at all the same information when he heard light, slow footsteps coming down the hall. King turned as the door opened.

"Midnight already?"

"It is." Dak had arrived as planned.

"Stick to the plan. You take her home and follow."

"And you're staying here? We need more than one set of eyes, unless you want me to bring in some guys."

Shit. King wanted distance, but he didn't want anyone other than Dak or himself involved until they knew what was going on. Dak was right. Or they wouldn't get to the bottom of this now. "No. This doesn't leave us. I'll leave after you and watch the street. You get the house."

"Good."

They locked the office behind them and went in search of Ember. Dak waited next to the fireplace. Ember's head lolled to the side, and the book had fallen to the floor. So much for not sleeping. Her inhale slightly louder than her exhale showed the beginnings of snoring. That didn't surprise him with the angle of her neck.

"Ember." He lowered his tone. She didn't stir. Trying again, he added a bite. "Ember."

Her breathing caught, but she didn't wake. He placed his

hand on her shoulder, the small frame fitting in his palm. "Ember."

A small moan preceded her fluttering eyes. Stiffening beneath him, she came to and took in her surroundings. Once she found him above her, she sighed.

"Time to go." King straightened and stepped back.

"Oh. Okay." Ember stood, stifling a yawn.

"He's taking you." King moved so that she could see Dak behind him.

"Oh." Trepidation brightened her eyes, and she looked at King. Her lips shook. He knew she hoped for something. But King didn't need to give it. He'd see her here again. One last time. King wouldn't return her after this.

Dak pushed off the mantle. "Let's go."

"Wait." King remembered as she took a step to follow him. Reaching into his back pocket, he pulled out the blindfold he'd grabbed from the office. "Wear this. Unless you want him to use your shirt." This time, he allowed his smirk to show and enjoyed her horrified gaze and pink cheeks.

Gripping her shoulders, he turned her around and nudged her toward Dak. Her bare feet padded across the wooden floor. With her head high, she met Dak's eyes as she walked past him. Dak quirked a brow and nodded at King before he left.

He had ten minutes to change and gather his things before he followed. Tonight, they would have answers.

5

———

"Will you tell me your name?" Ember's eyes quivered beneath the blindfold, moving at a pace to match her fearful heart rate. She didn't know this man. Not that she knew King, but this man wouldn't talk. Not a word. She tried. They'd been driving for a while. "My father's address..."

"I know where he lives." He cut her off, surprising her with the sudden, deep rumble of his voice in the car.

"Can I take the blindfold off now?" Silence fell again.

Moments later, the car stopped. Rough fingers at the back of her head released the blindfold. She winced to help her eyes adjust. He'd parked a block from her father's house, but in a different direction than King had the other night. No door-to-door service with this man, either. "So, thank you for the ride."

"Shirt."

"Excuse me?" Ember stopped reaching for the door handle and frowned at him.

"His shirt. Leave it here."

"Oh." She still wore King's shirt. She hesitated. But when

he raised his brow, he looked scarier than King. Ember peeled his shirt off without taking her pajama top with it. She dropped it on the seat behind her as she stepped from the car, not bothering to say bye to the man that didn't talk anyway.

Ember tiptoed across the pavement, aware of the small rocks, litter, and shards of glass. All the lights were out in her father's house. Letting herself in, she kept silent. She'd seen her father's car parked beside the house.

She paused. What was she thinking? Quiet? Arriving home after being kidnapped a second time, and she thought she needed to be quiet so as not to wake her father. They needed to do something this time. All the unknown and waiting had caught up to her. And it pissed her off.

The door swung shut with a thud and she turned on every light switch she passed. Hunger rolled in her belly. Safety of home allowed her some freedom. She had a plan. Eat, talk to her father, shower again, and put on the thickest sweatpants and sweatshirt she owned before going back to bed. No way was she going to be caught in thin pajamas around those men again. And in the morning, she was going to the police herself. King let her go. It wasn't up to him what she did now.

Maybe that should be her first stop rather than going to bed. But a few hours wouldn't make a difference. She wouldn't be taken again tonight. Whoever took her didn't know they had brought her home again. She had time to regroup.

Rushed thumps sounded down the stairs. Her father had a hand on the wall as he came around the corner.

"Ember?" Drowsiness didn't coat his voice like she'd expected. Of course, he wouldn't be asleep. He'd probably been worried about her.

"Hi, Dad. I'm home. After being kidnapped. Again." She couldn't keep the sarcasm from her voice while heating left-over lasagne she found in the fridge. She felt bad, though. None of this was her father's fault and he didn't deserve her snark. Slamming cupboard doors helped her let off some of her frustration.

"I don't understand."

"It's okay, Dad. I don't think I understand either." Ember walked over and hugged him. His arms came around her and squeezed her immediately. "But can we go to the police now?"

"I'm glad you're safe." He squeezed a little tighter before letting go and pulling away. "We'll go first thing in the morning. Tonight, we'll lock up and get some sleep."

Ember nodded and gave him a small smile before retrieving her plate from the microwave. Her father stood there, frowning, looking more exhausted than she'd ever seen him.

"I'm safe now, Dad. Why don't you go back to bed? I'm going to eat, shower, and go to bed myself."

"Okay, Ember." He leaned down and kissed her forehead before leaving. She told him she was safe, but she wasn't sure that was the truth.

Ember ate, then went upstairs to shower. Exhaustion forced her to be quick. In her dresser, she found a loose sweater that hung off one shoulder and her favourite sweat-pants that hugged her hips and flared for the length of the legs. She didn't care if she was too warm all night. Fully covered was her only option from now on.

THREE HOURS HAD PASSED since King had seen movement inside the house. Lights on in every room and Ember's figure storming through the place. A male had appeared minutes after she entered and he assumed it was Samuel Bellamy. There had been no more signs of movement since.

King didn't need to see Dak to know he was near. It was likely he'd broken into the house.

Red lights shone, and a car pulled out from beside the house. A black sedan he didn't recognize, but matched the make and model registered to Samuel Bellamy. King slid down in his seat as the car drove past. Dak appeared at the edge of the house. A quick nod of his head told King he needed to follow that car.

Remaining in the dark with no headlights, King stayed back as far as he could without losing them. Little traffic would make him easy to spot.

Bellamy pulled into a parking lot behind a restaurant. Few cars were scattered and parked for the night. Driving around the block, King parked on the corner of another street. Bellamy stood from his car and looked around, not making a move for about five minutes.

Ember's father opened the back seat and pulled out a limp body. Pain lanced through King's jaw. His entire body tightened with anger. Bellamy maneuvered his hold to open the back door of the car King had seen on his security footage.

Son of a bitch. King shook his head, following the car. He considered giving them a head start. Ember would be at his place when he got home. But he decided against it. Bellamy had tried twice to drop her off to King. If he planned to take her somewhere else since they'd returned her, King might not find her in time before she got hurt. King didn't like the churning in his gut at the thought of harm coming to her.

Bellamy turned toward King's property, and King continued past to back into the off-road path on the opposite side of the road. He waited until Bellamy returned and drove back to the city. With her father gone, King sped out of the path and up his lane to reach Ember. He found her in the same place as before. But this time, her clothes were different. A chuckle broke at the sight of her baggy sweats. Putting her in the backseat, he drove home.

He shouldn't like the familiarity of walking through the house with Ember in his arms. Stopping outside the spare bedroom, King hesitated. He inwardly cursed himself. One kiss with the girl and he wanted to lay her out on his bed and nowhere else. Slipping into his room, he set her down and covered her up. Keep her close. A better way to monitor her. As far as lies went, it was decent.

Dak returned as King entered the living room.

"Were you inside the house?"

"Not until after they left, but I was close enough to watch her room. Her father came in alone, then carried her out. I made it down to his car in time to see him leave with her unconscious. I went inside after." Dak's voice turned deadly. He didn't like what he'd found.

"He switched cars in the back parking lot of *Magma's Kitchen* and drove here."

"Think she'll believe us?" Dak raised a skeptical brow.

"I don't know. It still doesn't tell us why he keeps bringing her here." King couldn't guess the type of relationship Ember had with her father.

"I'll keep digging. Maybe a visit to dear daddy?" Dak asked.

"Soon."

"Got it. I'm hitting the hay." Dak walked past him and

toward the hall. He paused before disappearing. "Where is she?"

"My room."

Dak narrowed his eyes, saying without words his skepticism of King's decision. Shaking his head, he went to bed. King did the same. Sleep pulled at him. And he discovered a need to see that Ember was okay.

HER STOMACH TURNED. Ember didn't have to open her eyes to know what had happened. Her bed wasn't this firm. Staying still, on her back with her eyes closed, she recognized the malady running through her. More sedatives. If she opened her eyes, she'd have to face another day with so much unknown.

"You're awake." King's voice was quiet beside her.

"Mmm." She forced her eyes open and turned her head. King blurred in her vision and her head felt like it whipped around in a circle like a bobble-head doll. Dizziness swarmed behind her eyes, similar to the two previous times. King sat on the side of the bed. Darker bedding in a darker room. This must be his room. His bed. One of the rooms he'd made off limits. The espresso bed frame housed heavy sheets that weighed her down against the mattress. It resembled another cave inside his home.

She lifted the covers away from her. Forcing herself to look down, she sighed, letting her head fall back again. Thank God she wore her sweats to bed. King's chuckle sent a tremble through the mattress.

"I noticed your unique choice in pajamas."

"Mmm." She took slow, steady breaths to get rid of the

nausea. Dizziness she could deal with, but she didn't want to be sick, especially in front of King.

"Nauseous?"

"And dizzy." She winced. She sounded horrible.

"Side effects from the sedative he used. And from using it again so soon." The deeper voice that wasn't King's reverberated through the room. She tilted her head too quickly, causing an extra wave of dizziness. The man who'd taken her home stood in the doorway.

"Who?" She forced the word out, not sure if she was ready. Looking between both men, their hard expressions created an unease that only added to her nausea.

"We'll talk more when you're up and around. There's water on the nightstand for you. Come out when you can." King stood and followed the other man out of the room.

Did they catch whoever it was when they left her this time? She hoped so.

Ember took a deep breath and brought herself to a sitting position. It took her several minutes until she felt steady enough to lift the glass of water. Sipping it, she waited for the symptoms to dissipate long enough for her to make it to the bathroom. Splashing her face with cold water helped, and combing her hair gave her enough confidence to face the two men waiting for her.

Walking straight proved difficult, but Ember made it to the living room without falling on her face. King stood near the fire and the other man leaned against the wall, startling her as she came around the corner. Stepping away from him, she stopped.

"What do you know? And how?" Ember demanded with more confidence than she possessed.

"Come sit, Ember." King pointed to the chair she had

fallen asleep in last night. She obeyed, but only because she still felt a little groggy. "We followed you last night."

"You, too?" She'd thought King had stayed behind. Now it made sense why he'd asked Mr. Silent and Scary to take her.

"Yes. I watched and followed the car that left your father's house and he watched the house." King pointed to the man with no name.

"And?"

"It was your father." King had a distinct clear voice, but Ember must have heard him wrong.

"What? That doesn't make sense."

"I watched him go into your room myself." King's side-kick spoke.

"And who are you, anyway?" She snapped at him. He didn't flinch. He also didn't answer her. They seemed to only answer questions they wanted. "It wasn't my father." Ember looked back at King. "You were right. I shouldn't have trusted you. Why are you doing this? What do you want with me? Where is my father?"

"At the police station." King still wasn't answering her. The man against the wall that barely spoke a word answered her questions. "Filing a missing person's report for you. Report says he hasn't seen you for three days."

"Give me a phone." She demanded King.

"No."

"Fine. I'll just leave then." She stood and walked to the door, but when she saw King push off the wall, she broke into a run, an unsteady run. She didn't even make it within reach of the door before King plucked her off her feet, her arms trapped under his.

"You can't do that." King's calm voice warmed her ear, his breath brushing down the column of her neck.

"You mean you won't let me."

"That too. Now, are you going to sit back down, or do I have to restrain you?"

Ember sealed her lips. Not her father. These men were lying to her. Nausea swirled into a storm. Her attempt to run had been stupid. The drugs still ran their course through her body. But she didn't want to hear their lies. She'd trusted King. Her own stupid mistake. King told her not to.

Her father loved her. They'd always been so close. The thought of him doing this to her made her numb.

King sighed and set her down in front of the chair, not backing away until Ember sat down again.

"I also saw your father pull you from the back of his car to switch cars. The same car that has been showing up on my security footage. And I followed him here." Ember just kept shaking her head as King talked.

"I want to go back to bed." Ember rubbed her hand across her forehead. Terrified and defeated, Ember had no choice. King hadn't harmed her.

She stood and King grabbed her arm, his grip tight. This touch was nothing like the last. Power poured from him.

"Don't try to leave, Ember." Ember flinched from the danger in his voice. Her memory flashed back to her first night here. This was the man that did bad things and did them well. This was a man to fear.

Ember stayed silent and waited for his grip to loosen.

"Back in my room." King released her arm. He'd directed her to the last place she wanted to be, but arguing wouldn't be wise. She recognized the difference in him now.

She closed his bedroom door and looked for a lock, finding one on the inside. After turning it, she lay down on the bed. Tears tried to rise, clogging her vision. Ember clenched her jaw to hold them back. To hold the fear back.

They had to be wrong--a misunderstanding. Her father promised her they'd go to the police this morning. That's where she should be right now, with him. He'd promised her. But she disappeared again before they could. Seeing her father each night had given her a false sense of safety. And with King.

But for the first time in her life, doubt in her father crawled through her like a snake. And she hated the man that put it there.

6

———

He'd expected Ember's reaction. Her denial. Her stubborn belief in her father. When someone had a present and caring parent or two, why would they abandon their belief in them? But he hadn't expected her to run. King looked at Dak who'd been frowning down the hall.

"You're staying for now. She doesn't leave this house. Once she's accepted that it was her father, we can give her some space, but for now, she has one of us on her at all times. We need to find out why he keeps bringing her here."

"You trust her?" Dak asked, familiar skepticism sharpening his glare.

"Yeah. Don't ask me to explain why." King pinched the bridge of his nose. Frustration welled against his own instincts.

"I bet I could think of a reason." Dak's implication straightened King's spine.

"Careful where you're going with that, Dak."

"She's a pretty piece of ass." Dak never questioned King before, yet now he taunted him. King tolerated little, more so with Dak because of their close history, but even he understood what he'd said went too far. King took two steps to square off with his friend.

"Has a *pretty piece of ass* ever got in my way before?" No. Nothing ever stopped King.

"You're retired now." Dak shrugged. The thought King had turned weak because of his choice pissed him off.

"I'm still the same man." Deadly intent rang through every word.

Dak's lips twitch. "Just checking." He turned down the hall toward the bedrooms.

What the fuck was that? King admitted his attraction to Ember. But he also had to admit Dak had a point. He didn't chase women around with his dick, but neither had he ever treated a woman the way he had Ember. It would be a mistake to allow that attraction to rule. Just as the kiss and his attitude the day before had been a mistake. No excuse came forth. But his attraction didn't affect his belief in her innocence. He'd made that conclusion before he ever laid a hand on her.

King needed space and in a place where all he had was space, he only found solace in the security office. An hour of watching the footage on repeat gave him nothing new. The only difference in the last video being when King drove up after Ember's father. Why King? Why did Bellamy bring his daughter to him?

Damn it. The quickest way to find out information would be to corner Bellamy, but King wasn't ready to draw attention to himself or step into a trap. Traps he could handle. They were easy to twist to his advantage with enough information. But they didn't have enough information to step on the trigger. They needed to monitor the investigation into Ember's kidnapping.

King stretched and rolled his neck, looking backward at

the door. Only a short distance separated him from Ember. Would he find her awake or sleeping off the rest of the sedatives? Dak still stood in the hall, guarding the door.

"Go gather information about the investigation. I've got her." King motioned for Dak to leave.

"Door was locked." He pushed off the wall.

"Meaning you already picked the lock."

"Yup." Dak left and King let himself into his room. Ember laid on her side with the covers tucked up to her chin and her dark waves spilled over the pillows. Slow breathing lifted her shoulder as the sedatives tried to leave her system. He should let her sleep, yet found himself beside her, stroking her hair back from her face. For a father who loved his daughter, he didn't seem to attach much value to her.

Ember stirred. Green glistened as her eyes fluttered open. "King?" For one unguarded moment, the green in her eyes softened. It didn't last. Looking down, she shrunk away, pulling the covers with her as she moved closer to the centre of the bed and propped up her shoulders.

"Still don't believe me?" He inched closer, not allowing the space she'd tried to take.

"I don't know what to believe." Sleep still lingered in her voice, pulling her emotions to the surface. "But I'm scared."

"We had to take you home to follow your kidnapper. I don't understand what your father is up to." King had a feeling there was a deeper threat involved, but was that a threat to him, or her? "Ember." He paused, dropping her name to coax her to look at him again. "You can't leave here until I figure this out."

"Are you still saying you didn't take me?" So much courage peered through her glassy eyes, trying to look past his barrier, his shield.

"I didn't take you." He let his sincerity through.

"Are you going to hurt me?" Her jaw quivered with the effort to keep herself contained while asking that question. King reached out and traced her cheek with his index finger.

"What do you think?" Any answer he gave would only be words.

"You could." Her fists clutched at the blankets, and her breath stalled in her chest.

"You're right, but will I?" Despite the beliefs of the king of mercenaries, he didn't harm the innocent if it was in his power.

"No," she whispered.

"No, I won't hurt you." King cupped her jaw and leaned in. "I might do other things, though." He paused inches from her lips, waiting for her to back away in fear. She didn't. With hooded eyes, King watched her tongue dart out to lick her lips. Her breathing turned shallow and her eyes lowered to his mouth. No, he didn't scare her.

He moved in the last few inches and took control of her mouth. Tilting her jaw for better access, he pushed her back against the headboard, letting her feel some of his weight. Delicate and feminine, despite the baggy clothing. Her lips moved with his. His hands burned with the urge to touch bare skin, to reach under her clothes.

Ember's hands fluttered up, landing on his shoulders. Her fingertips applied pressure, but she didn't give any push or pull.

Two firm taps echoed from the other side of the door before it opened. Ember tensed, and she pulled her hands away. King blocked her with his body and turned his head over his shoulder. Dak hadn't waited for acceptance before opening the door. He stood expressionless in the hall.

"She needs to see this." Once they both stood, Dak

turned back to the living room. Ember lagged behind King as she toed her way down the hall. Dak restarted the paused news conference when Ember's eyes locked onto her father on the screen.

"Please. If you've taken my daughter, return her. Turn yourself in. I just want my girl back. I haven't seen her for three days, since she left for her morning run. Please." Bellamy pleaded to the assembled crowd outside the police station. King looked between Ember and her father as he lied in front of hundreds. Her father's speech seemed sincere, but there was something off about his performance. Worry and grief were there, but there was more. He looked afraid.

"Three days?" Ember whispered. "But I just saw him last night, and the entire day before. And I don't run. Why would he lie?"

"Because there's more to this. Something or someone else is involved." King sighed. "Ember, you can't leave and I'm not taking you home again."

Ember swiped at damp trails on her cheeks. "I know." Her quiet acceptance almost broke him. The man who raised her, a daughter's hero, betrayed her.

"Do we leave?" Dak lifted his chin, looking at King over Ember's head. In the past, moving locations would be the first course of action.

"Not yet." King wouldn't rule it out. But he'd built this place hoping to have something permanent for himself. "I'll give her a proper tour of the house today. This is still the safest place to be for now." His home wasn't what it seemed.

"WILL you do as you're told?" The warning lacing King's voice sent a tremor through Ember's body. She recognized the distinct vibrations. If she didn't obey him, he'd take away the freedom she'd had the day before.

She nodded. "Yes, I will."

King tilted his head. His narrowed eyes froze the air in her lungs. She held on as the pressure seemed to increase. At the point Ember shook, her gaze wavering, he nodded. "Okay. If anyone other than one of us steps on this property, you hide. I'm going to show you where. He'll hide with you." King nodded to the other man.

"I still don't know who *he* is." But King just kept talking instead of introducing him. Not that she expected answers from either of them.

"If he can't get to you right away, he will find you."

"If someone is going to come looking for me, why would I hide?" If they found her unharmed, she could go home and all would be well.

Not home.

"Because you may not be the one they're looking for." His implication dawned on her.

"You think my father is trying to set you up? That's ridiculous!" She cringed at her high-pitched outburst. But a thread of denial hissed in her mind.

"I'm not taking chances."

Ember sighed. No matter the scenario, she was a damn pawn. Hell, her father not only allowed it, but had kidnapped her himself. "So, now what?"

"I'll show you the hiding places. Then, we wait."

"Of course we just wait." Ember mumbled over rolling irritation. A waiting game while she sorted through the emotions of being used by her father.

"Come on." King turned, expecting her to follow. She

hesitated as the other man walked past her. He ducked his head to her ear.

"Dak." He straightened, and she looked at him in time to see him wink. A name. Ember nodded once, trying not to smile with the confidence knowing both their names gave her. She followed King.

King went from room to room, starting in the kitchen with the trapdoor at the back of a coat closet, then the study with a small hidden room behind a shelf that worked as both a hiding spot and an exit to outside. King stopped outside the bathroom next.

"You can escape through the window in here, but that is a last resort. Only use it if you can't get to any of the other escapes."

"Why?"

"It's easy to track and rather obvious." King waited for her to nod before continuing down the hall. His house had a hidey hole or an escape in almost every room. A hatch led to a hidden attic, more like a flat crawl space. King pushed the hatch back into place, the cracks of the door disappearing. The last to show her was the exit in the floor of his bedroom. That one also led to an escape tunnel. They stopped in the hall outside the locked door.

"What about that room?" The one he'd warned her away from. His eyes narrowed for a moment before he gave a small nod.

Pulling a key from his pocket, he unlocked the door. She hadn't been sure what to expect, but a small scale security office hadn't been it.

"Wow." She looked across all the screens, five across a desk the length of the back wall. A few displayed the house and others showed the property outside.

"Here's where I found you each time." He pointed to the

far left screen. "It's inside the trees at the end of the lane, inside the perimeter line. Just enough that it sounds the alarm. Five hundred metres from the house."

"My dad just left me there?" Ember tried to picture it, tried to imagine her father drugging her and dumping her in the woods. She heard King breathe in, but he didn't answer her. She looked up at him. "Is it on tape? Do you have a video of my father leaving me there?" Her anger clogged her throat.

"I do," King answered.

"Show it to me. Please." Ember couldn't temper her demand. She needed to see what her father looked like abandoning his drugged daughter in the woods. King's expression never changed. He waited. "Please."

"Okay." King sat down in front of the monitor closest to him and clicked through files. A new window popped up, and a video started playing. A car she didn't recognize drove up, making a quick U-turn to face away from the house and away from the camera. The man was unidentifiable dressed from head to toe in black, but his build and walk resembled her father's in a way she couldn't ignore.

Oh Dad. Why? The image of the man Ember looked up to with all her heart crumbled away as cracks spread. Her father was a good man. There had to be a reason.

He opened the back door and pulled Ember out. Her arms hung down and her head lolled backward, too limp to only be asleep. The video showed her in shorts and a tank top--this was the first night he left her. Her father laid her down on the ground and ran back to the car, leaving a cloud of dust dissipating after he drove off.

"Are there..." She had to clear her throat and swallow before she continued. "Are there videos from the other nights?"

"Yes, but they're the same as this."

"Show me?"

King didn't hesitate this time. It bothered her to watch this, but she needed to. She needed to see what she didn't know.

The videos were practically identical. Her father paused before leaving the second time, and she wore different clothes in each video.

King turned off the screen and stood. Her body shivered as he towered over her.

"What did you do? To need all these secret exits and this kind of security?" Ember swallowed down her nerves through her croaked whisper. Tilting her head, she watched his eyes glaze over.

"I'm just cautious."

"Bullshit." She didn't say it with any heat. Calling out a man like King on his lies held a high risk, but she wanted to feel safe with him. "That might be true, but that isn't why."

He tilted his chin down. "I've told you before. Be careful what you ask."

Ember bit the inside of her lip and turned her head, chastened. She wanted to press him, make him answer her. His finger under her chin lifted her head. She thought he was going to tell her, but he was shaking his head. His thumb came up and the touch under her chin tightened to a firm grip. He didn't show any warning before he took her mouth. His lips moving and parting hers. Ember softened and accepted him in without thought. She granted him access, enjoying the slide of his tongue over hers. This was a moment to let go. A moment to escape into something else. Into someone else. It may not be the right thing to do, but Ember embraced it.

King deepened the kiss as he moved his hands around

her to cup her ass. The kiss muffled her shriek when he lifted her, pinning her against the wall beside the door. She locked her ankles together behind him. Fire lanced in thick lines under her sweater from the touch of his fingers on her bare skin, gliding until his thumb rubbed over her nipple. Their lips never broke while he took her breast in his hand, pressing the nipple to his palm and kneading. She gasped, giving him an advantage to tilt her head and devour more of her.

Sensitive skin lit up her body with heat pooling in all the right places. A kiss of passion like this wasn't on her resume. Her body reacted not only to the kiss or his touch, but to a man with the name of King capable of terrible things.

A clearing throat near her ear sent her body into a rigid state. Ember tried to get out of King's hold, but he didn't pull back. He only slowed his movements, ending the kiss in his own time, and returned his hand to her hip.

"You need food and a few supplies. I came to ask how you wanted to handle that, but you have her covered."

"Wait!" Ember wiggled, forcing King to release her, and Dak stopped. "Supplies? Can I get some things?" She looked between the two of them.

"That depends what it is. There can't be anything here to give someone reason to think you've been here," King explained.

"A change of clothes? Bra? Underwear?" Material things didn't appease her. Makeup and hair products weren't things she used daily.

"What?" Both men asked at the same time.

King cursed. "Fuck."

That would leave a trace of a woman here, but any woman, not specifically her. Nonetheless, it posed a problem.

"No. If there's something you can't do without, we'll get it then. But for now, nothing."

"Are you serious? Not even a change of clothes? Some underwear? How would anyone know it isn't just a girlfriend of yours?"

"No." His answer slashed low and hard. When she thought passion had pinned them to the wall, it had been the hard and devastating man in front of her that had devoured her.

"I'll be back soon." Dak left them glaring at each other.

"I wish you'd told me all this last night before taking me home. Easy enough to wear an extra layer as a spare. Maybe I could have taped some necessities to my torso to ensure I'd have what I need during my stay after being kidnapped!" She stepped back, letting her sarcasm rule.

His arms crossed his chest, his broad chest that had helped pin her to the wall in the best damn kiss of her life. "You could have tried, but you wouldn't have had any of it for very long."

"You bastard." Her glowing hatred in her whisper darkened his face to a menacing shadow.

"Careful, little girl."

Emotions clashed within her, fear and anticipation. She was almost mad enough to call him out on it, almost curious enough to see what he'd do. He promised he wouldn't hurt her. Could she handle it? With one more heartbeat, Ember realized she wasn't ready to find out. She turned on her heel before she challenged him further and regretted it.

King flexed his fingers and his cock raged. If he hadn't seen more than irritation in her eyes, he would have slammed her back against the wall and continued where they left off. It had been a long time since someone stood up to him like Ember. Shaking it off, he sat back down to watch her on the monitors. She stopped in the living room, her body vibrating as she turned in a circle. Tense jaw and fire in her eyes. It didn't last. After a moment, her anger deflated. Her body sagged without enough energy to hold herself up.

He shouldn't care. He shouldn't have pinned her to the wall. And he shouldn't be watching her for any other reason than to make sure she didn't run. But his gaze traced her slim form that hid beneath the sweats. Her smooth skin and palm-sized breasts. As she shuffled toward the chair near the fire and pulled the blanket from the couch on her way, King fought with himself to go in there and hold her. She was supposed to be an inconvenience.

Ember plopped in the chair, bringing her feet beneath her, and tucked the blanket under her chin. The video didn't give a clear image of her face turned toward the fire, but

King imagined how her eyes had changed from anger to defeat. Glossy and desperate for answers.

Why hadn't he locked her in a room until he got rid of her? He'd developed a soft spot for the girl, one he'd never allowed himself to have before. He left the office. Stopping in the hall, his gaze landed on the small lump she created in the chair. He wanted to say something, but when he opened his mouth, nothing came out.

"Just leave me alone, King." The weary sound almost didn't reach him.

"Not for long, Ember." But King didn't know if he'd said that because he wanted to be near her or because she was the bait left out for the taking in this scheme and needed to get used to him and Dak being near.

While he worried what was coming, he felt an eagerness he hadn't known was missing. For the first time in two years, he considered his retirement may have been too soon.

No. He'd been right to get out of that world. His dark and oily soul couldn't take any more.

The other night was the first time in months since he'd called Dak for anything. Since King retired, they didn't discuss business. There were times Dak showed up for a few hours or a few days and the two of them barely spoke a word to each other.

Well, hell. All of this was forcing King to crawl out of a hole he hadn't known he'd been in.

King sat at his desk in his study, moving paper and making calls that didn't need to be made, until the alarm alerted him of Dak driving back up the lane.

Ember hadn't moved.

"Ember," King started, but Dak interrupted him by coming through the door.

"Pizza." He shouldered his way in with several bags in one hand and balancing the pizza box on the other.

"Let's go." King stood in front of Ember, tilting his head to where Dak disappeared into the kitchen.

"No. Thank you. I'm no..." Her stomach interrupted her. She sighed. "I'm fine. I'd rather stay here."

"That wasn't a request. You're done being alone. Come eat." Her eyes snapped up to his, lit with fire. Good. It was better than sulking.

"Fine." Mild petulance drew out the word. King waited for her to pass him, then followed her into the kitchen. Dak turned the box toward Ember, who plopped herself down at the island. King reached in front of her to help himself, making sure his body brushed against hers.

No one spoke, but when King looked at Dak, he was staring at Ember.

"What is it?" King asked.

"What's the connection?" He glanced at King before his gaze landed back on Ember.

"Million dollar question." The one that would answer it all.

"Money?" Dak frowned.

"Hmm. I don't think so." King had nothing to go on but instinct.

"My father doesn't need money." Ember straightened, matching her posture to her defensive tone.

"You know that for sure, sweetheart?" Dak raised a brow at her.

"Don't call me sweetheart." Even the little thing that she was could put menace behind her words. She'd shown some spine so far.

"I'm just saying. You never thought your own father would kidnap you. Do you know him so well?" Dak taunted her, forcing her to rethink her relationship with her father. King watched it play out. It needed to be done. Better Dak than him.

Her jaw tensed. "My father and I have always been close. We tell each other everything." She paused. "Or we did, until now." No longer did she hold on to her outright refusal of her father's actions, but hadn't yet accepted them. A glare aiming at Dak, intending to seem deadly, only appeared cute on the tiny woman. "You're an asshole."

"I'm worse than that, sweetheart." She wasn't in good company.

"I'm going to bed." Pushing the pizza box further away from her, she stood. King grabbed her elbow as she passed. "Could you please stop doing that?" Warm eyes landed on his hand wrapped around her arm.

"I doubt I'll stop touching you." He lowered his voice, not to keep Dak from hearing, but to see the effect it had on her. Ember's hitched breath brought her closer to him. King needed to know she was still attracted to him, that their moment in the office hadn't been a one off. He needed to know that despite her anger, that when he kissed her again, she wouldn't push him away.

"Can I sleep in the same spare room as before?" She tore her eyes away and looked over his shoulder.

"My room."

"What?" she squeaked and her green gaze fell to his.

"You'll be sleeping in my room again."

"Why?"

King looked up, pretending to consider it, still holding her arm. "That's a good question." One he didn't want to answer.

He let go and tilted his head behind him, telling her to

go ahead. She only paused to look between him and Dak before leaving. Once she was gone, King spoke.

"We need to find that connection."

"Easier said than done," Dak drawled.

"If we can't figure it out soon, pay Bellamy a visit."

"You got it." Dak grabbed his third slice of pizza, but King wanted to ask him one last question.

"What are your thoughts on Ember now?"

"She's cute." King frowned at Dak. That was the last thing he expected to hear. "And she's a pawn." Dak left, not seeing King nod. King didn't have to worry how Dak would treat Ember while they had her. And he wasn't sure why that mattered to him.

SPARKS SEETHED through her body from King's touch. The heat from each finger sent off small streams of fire that never died. And his voice. That deep hum made her throb. Frustrations roared inside her when she couldn't control her body's reaction to the man's touch but she wanted to slap both him and Dak, scream at her father and beat the person responsible for all of this--assuming those weren't the same people. For hours, with every hum, thrum, throb, and humph, Ember flopped herself into a new position in bed. Storming out of the kitchen hadn't given her any other option than to go to bed too early.

The numbers on the clock rolled to a single one and her neck, shoulders, and head ached from the lack of true rest. She tensed to change positions once again, but froze when the door opened. Slumping against the mattress, Ember slowed her breathing.

"You can stop pretending." King's too deep voice didn't

bounce around the room. She huffed and rolled over. The moon lit the bedroom more than any lamp might have. His shirt dropped to the floor, and he reached for the zipper of his jeans. Instinct made her slap her hand over her eyes and roll back over.

"I'm sorry."

"For what?"

"For looking. I didn't know you were undressing." She'd rolled away too soon in her opinion, what with the way the light showed every indent of muscle and made his tattoos move like shadows.

"I'm not shy." The bed dipped. "Roll over, Ember." His steady cadence smoothed her nerves. Yet, she only peeked over her shoulder, her hand still at the ready to block her sight. He was naked except for black boxer briefs. His large hand settled on her shoulder and pulled her onto her back.

"King?" Ember tried to keep her eyes upward, but each time his eyes dipped lower, she followed suit. "Why am I here? I mean, in your room?"

He pulled her blocking-ready hands away from her face and leaned forward. "Because I'm keeping you close. And this is where I want you."

"But, why?" The why was important to her.

"Do you need an answer to that?" His mouth formed a flat line, as if the answer was obvious.

"Maybe." Did she need him to verbalize what she felt when he touched her?

King tilted his head. He braced his hands on either side of her and leaned closer. She shivered. Minty heat brushed over her chin and cheek from his breath.

Ember swallowed, needing to think fast. Would he let her push him away? Did she want to? Would he stop if she asked him to? He'd warned her of what kind of man he was.

He hadn't forced himself on her earlier, but neither had he given her a choice.

"I don't have an answer." His lips captured hers and she embraced the familiar yet foreign touch. She knew this kiss, but what it could do to her was a mystery she might not be ready for. Ember placed her hands on his chest and pushed. Lifting himself up, he froze for a moment before raising his brow.

"Just checking something."

King smirked. He'd seen through her test. This time when he kissed her, he glided one hand under her sweater. She didn't forget for a moment his warning. Even one of his hands was deadly. Adrenaline sparked something dangerous inside her. One hand, one touch, and Ember wanted more. He reached her breast and her back bowed. Rough circles around her nipple had her panting. He rolled the nub between his thumb and finger, increasing the pressure with each pass.

It was startling how easily she opened up to King. With any other man, Ember turned into some awkward person, unable to be herself in the bedroom. But with King, a man no one should put this kind of trust in--effortless.

Dropping to his elbow, King shifted his other hand to skate over her hip to the waist of her sweatpants. She hated wearing these clothes. That thought alone jolted her simmering anger at being denied something as simple as a change of clothes. For God's sake, a pair of underwear. She supposed she only had herself to blame for not wearing underwear to bed.

King squeezed her nipple hard enough to make her gasp. "Don't get away from me now, girl." Hard and smooth, his voice brought her back to the moment. Any other person, and Ember would hate the condescending way he said *girl*. But King turned the word into something different.

His hand continued its path until his finger reached the hood above her clitoris. Everything in her froze, waiting. Wanting to know what it would be like, what he could do to her. When he touched and applied pressure, her lips opened in a silent gasp.

He broke the kiss. "Been a while?"

Ember let out a half laugh, a humourless one, unsure how to answer that. "Not really. It's just... This is just..." Bright idea to tell the man with which she had a complete disadvantage that he affected her like no other.

He circled her clit before moving down to her entrance. One circle and slowly and steadily, he pushed into her. Ember lost her ability to think. Her knees opened more on their own and she moved her head back until King caught her in another kiss and curled his finger inside her. It built. So much all in her core. She held back her moan for more.

As if he read her mind, he added a second finger, stretching her. Her hips lifted in invitation. King held her lips captive, yet she had the urge to bite them. Ember nipped his bottom lip instead. His growl vibrated down her throat, and he pressed his thumb to her clit.

A knock registered through the haze in her ears. King lifted his head, and his working hands paused.

"Son of a bitch." Ember cursed in half a breath. King snapped his head back, his eyes wide with surprise. "What?" she asked.

He chuckled before pulling his hands out from under her clothes and sitting up. "What is it?" His calm voice bothered Ember. If he had been as affected as she, he wouldn't be welcoming the intrusion.

Dak opened the door. He didn't speak, but jerked his

head outward for King to step out. King sighed and looked down at Ember again.

"Sorry. You go to sleep." He stood.

"Should I come?" Ember moved to sit up.

"No." King was putting his jeans back on. "Go to sleep." And he left.

"Son of a bitch is right. The bastard." Ember cursed again after he left. So damn easy for him to just pull away, leaving her with a need like she'd never experienced before. This was probably just an average Tuesday for him. He wasn't affected by her any more than he would be another random woman. How convenient to have one here to play with for a little while. Cold chilled her veins, sobering her up fast.

"WHAT IS IT?" King growled when he followed Dak into the security office, having left Ember in bed, on the verge of an all-consuming climax.

"We might have a visitor."

"Might?" Dak pointed to the monitor showing the same car Bellamy used to drop off Ember each night backing away from his property and stopping before driving forward again, always stopping before he crossed the perimeter that would set off his alarm.

"He's been doing that for five minutes. I was about to call it a night when the car pulled up on the monitor." Dak looked straight at King. "He knows where the property line is."

"I can see that." King could take the opportunity and confront Bellamy now, scare him off and let him wonder what King had done with his daughter, or ignore him and wait for him to leave on his own. But Bellamy only sat there for another minute before backing up again, and this time he kept going. "Looks like daddy has a conscience."

"King, he isn't the one running this."

"No. But what father sends his daughter to the most dangerous man known?" That man knew what kind of danger he put his daughter in when he left her here. King had his own standards, but they weren't well known. He also earned the title of King. "You call it a night. I've got this."

Dak yawned as he left, leaving King in the dim room. If the man came back, King would grab him.

8

King tracked Ember under hooded eyes as she slipped from the bed and tiptoed into the bathroom. He'd returned after more than an hour with no sign of Bellamy again. The shower started, prompting King out of bed and into the other bathroom for a shower of his own. He'd finished and was cooking breakfast when Ember walked in. King had to do a double take.

"Are those my boxers?" Rolled at the waist, they looked like loose exercise shorts. She wore one of his T-shirts tied in a knot at her hip. It still hung below her hip on the side she hadn't tied.

"Yes, they are." Tilting her head up, she pointed to her challenge with her nose in the air. "I need to wash the clothes I do have. Do you have a problem with that?"

"I do," he drawled.

"What else am I supposed to do?"

King set down the spatula and turned on Ember. Her green eyes sparked, but her feet settled further apart. "Watching your tone would be one." He ran the back of his knuckles down the front of her--his--shirt, where it settled against her breast. Her nipple pebbled against the cotton. King didn't know what to do with someone who gave him attitude. No one ever dared before. If they did, they didn't last long.

Her face paled compared to the flush high in her cheeks. She recognized the warning, but she didn't back down. Pulling in a breath, she held it in between pinched lips. She stepped around him and sat herself down on the same stool she'd used each time.

King turned back around and flipped the next pancake, keeping Ember in his peripheral vision. Dak lumbered into the kitchen and went straight for the coffee pot. He poured himself a cup and drank it black, wincing at the temperature. King had a pile of pancakes sitting beside him. Dak pulled down a couple of plates after setting his mug on the island. He put two pancakes on one and the last three on the other, passed the two to Ember and set his plate beside her. He grabbed forks and the syrup from the fridge, then sat down.

King inwardly shook his head at the scene. He'd been so used to living alone, happy with the quiet. Having Dak make himself at home and Ember standing up to him left him perplexed.

"What happened last night?" Ember's voice broke the silence that blanketed the kitchen.

"Nothing to worry about." King took the last pancake out of the pan.

"But what was it?" Ember looked at Dak when King didn't answer again, but Dak only raised his brow at her before continuing to eat. He knew better than to say anything.

She didn't need to know her father still had a conscience. Yet.

He fixed his own plate and poured his second cup of coffee.

"What do we do today?" She'd finished eating and took the coffee pot from King. When he didn't answer, she paused. "Seriously? Nothing?"

"You're free to do what you normally do, as long as you do it here. And in your own clothes." But King couldn't wait to wear that shirt.

"I can't."

"Why is that?" King cut another bite of his pancakes and put it in his mouth.

"I don't have my guitar and other than that, I don't stay inside all day."

"Guitar, huh? I wouldn't mind hearing that." Behind her snippy tone and frustration, King watched her cheeks pinken. He hid his grin and continued. "I'm sorry, but you'll have to make do here. Use the TV and there's lots to read and there's the exercise equipment in the back bedroom if you need to work off some energy."

Ember ran her fingers over her forehead, then through her hair. Her frustration shook through her sigh, but she wasn't making this difficult for him, despite not knowing the dangers he could invoke.

"Yeah." Ember left, her shoulders straight. It was hard to admit to himself he didn't want to see Ember hurt.

EMBER FINISHED the laundry and put her sweats back on, grinning as she folded his boxers and shirt. She'd enjoyed the look on King's face when he realized she was wearing his clothes, but then that voice of his deepened, a warning she approached dangerous territory. Part of her wanted to know exactly what he'd do. She had to remind herself that he told her he wasn't a good man. But he'd been kind to her, mostly.

Except last night. His casual attitude when he'd pulled away and left replayed in her mind. Ember had a hard time remembering she was nothing new to him.

Ember roamed the house aimlessly, passing Dak or King a time or two. King always touched her when they passed-- fingers, his shoulder, even his breath. She needed to make herself stationary, and fast. He didn't need more encouragement, and neither did she.

She found the book she'd started still in the living room on an end table. Mentally shrugging, she picked it up. Ember curled back up in the same seat with the blanket. It took her a little while to find her place since she'd fallen asleep reading it, but once she did, the mystery of the widow's murdered sister-in-law dragged her back.

Hours passed and Ember walked down the dark hall of her husband's family home. The creaking of a rocking chair coming from the room at the end. It was all too predictable, so Ember didn't understand why shivers ran down her arms. She reached for the knob and turned. Her husband, who'd been dead for two years, was tied to the rocking chair. Ember rushed into the room. Chaos broke. A shrill shriek from a woman resembling a banshee came from behind the door. The door slammed shut and the maniacal woman charged toward her.

A hand came down on Ember's shoulder and she screamed, using the book to hit the woman attacking her.

King grabbed her wrist and stopped her attack. Ember let out a breath she didn't know had stuck in her lungs.

"Easy there. Good book?" He didn't loosen his grip and the heat sunk into her skin to push away the shivers still running up and down her arm. "I said your name twice. You didn't hear me?"

"No. Time to put the book down, I guess." She took in another breath, steadying herself. "You were trying to get my attention?"

"I was asking if you were hungry." King released her wrist. "You didn't come out for lunch."

"I didn't? What time is it?" Ember frowned and looked around the room for a clock, but didn't see one.

"Six." King's lips were twitching.

"Seriously? Yeah, time to put the book down." Ember bent the corner of the page and set the book back on the end table. She stood up, intending to follow King to the kitchen, but he didn't move. Swaying, she worked to keep her balance in front of him.

He slid his fingers to the underside of her wrist. One side of his mouth turned up. "Your pulse is still racing."

"Turns out the book isn't as predictable as I thought."

"The best things never are." His smile disappeared, but he brought her wrist up to his lips. Dark eyes locked with hers when he kissed over her pulse, his lips warm against the chills on her skin.

He released her and turned, walking to the kitchen. The chills turned to a direct line of heat that raced up her arm, then down to her core. How could he affect with such ease, then just let it go and walk away? She wished she reacted to him like she did any other man–difficult and awkward. Keeping her distance would be easy. He'd read her awkward behavior as disinterest.

She forced herself to follow King. When she walked in, Dak held up his phone.

"Another press conference." He tapped the screen and set it down on the island so she and King could see it.

"I'm willing to offer a reward if you turn yourself in. Please, don't harm my daughter. The police have been working around the clock to find out who took her. They will look favourably on you if you come forward yourself. And I will give you a reward for returning her unharmed." Her father spoke clearly throughout his entire speech. Then he stepped back and a police officer took over.

Seeing her father pleading at a press conference when he knew exactly where he'd taken his daughter churned the acid in her empty stomach. What other parts of himself had he kept hidden from her? Her dad had always been her hero until yesterday, when she first saw him lie to the entire country on television.

"I'm not hungry." Ember left the kitchen, not able to stomach watching more and not able to stomach food either. She went back to her book, starting over from where the main character walked down the dark hall, giving the story a chance to immerse her again rather than seeing her father's face in her mind or feeling his arms hug her and tell her he was glad she was safe.

KING'S EYES popped open when he heard the low squeak of his bedroom door. His body on alert and ready, he saw the empty space beside him. Ember. He sat up and reached for the jeans he'd left on the floor and buttoned them on the way out of his room. Practiced silence moved him through the house in Ember's wake. King doubted she'd do something foolish. The kitchen light shone into the living room. He stopped at the entrance and leaned against the arch. The wall chilled his bare shoulder.

Ember pulled the leftover pizza from the night before

out of the fridge. She put a single slice on a plate and into the microwave. Crossing her arms as if to hug herself, she turned. The moment she spotted him, her hands flew to her chest, and she jumped with a muffled scream.

"Oh my God! Make some noise!" Dark shadows rounded her wide eyes.

"Couldn't sleep?" King pushed off the wall and walked into the kitchen.

"No, I was hungry." She lowered her hand and relaxed against the counter until the microwave beeped.

"Not eating will have that effect."

She pulled out her plate and started eating large bites as her stomach rumbled low. King let her eat in silence, pouring them both glasses of water. When she finished, Ember put her plate in the sink and leaned against the counter. Her eyes had locked onto a random spot on the floor across the kitchen.

"I used to know everything about my father. At least I thought I did. Now, I'm questioning it all. And I hate that. I'm questioning vacations while I was growing up I'm analyzing every little conversation we've had and every decision he's made." She chewed on the inside of her cheek. "I'm still not sure I would have believed you if I hadn't seen him lie during the press conference. He was adamant that we didn't go to the police after you returned me home the first time. I think a part of me is still hoping that there is a good explanation."

"An explanation for drugging and kidnapping his own daughter?" King stopped himself from adding that her father had to know who he gave his daughter to, a very dangerous man.

"There has to be a reason. He wouldn't or couldn't..." She stopped, unable to finish.

"I'm sure there is." He refrained from telling her it likely wasn't an acceptable one. King stepped in front of her and tucked her hair behind her ear, letting the black silk run through his fingers as he pulled his hand back.

"But? There's something you're not saying, right?"

He searched her face. King didn't want to be the final nail in the coffin that completely tore her away from the only family she had.

"Ember, there aren't many situations where someone would give a person they care about to me for safety."

"There aren't many? Meaning there are some?" Her hope might be cracked, but she still held onto the pieces.

"Rare cases. But in a situation like this, they wouldn't expect you to come out the other side hale and whole."

"Then why haven't you?" She tilted her head back. With no fear in her eyes, this innocent girl asked why he hadn't hurt her. He pried open her arms and pressed his body to hers, trapping her against the counter. Her pulse increased, throbbing at the base of her exposed neck.

"People make assumptions that aren't always right. And this." King leaned down and took her lips. As soon as he made contact, he knew he wouldn't stop this time. Wouldn't stop from seeing or feeling her skin or stop from burying himself deep inside her. He gripped her hips and rocked himself against her, letting her feel how this would end.

She gasped and pulled back. "I wondered."

"Wondered what?"

Her cheeks reddened under his scrutiny. No way would he let her evade the question now.

"Ember?"

"I had wondered if this even affected you, or if I affected you." She murmured.

"What would make you think that?" He ground against her to reinforce the issue.

"You can turn it all off and walk away."

King chuckled low. "I am anything but unaffected by you, girl."

"Oh." She wouldn't meet his eyes.

"Now you're holding something back. What is it?"

"This is usually difficult and awkward for me."

King shook his head. "I don't follow."

"This," she gestured between them, "has always been awkward. I've accepted that about myself."

King let his hands glide under her clothes, one resting on her bare hip and the other delving lower to spread her folds, her wet folds. "Are you feeling awkward now?"

"No, and that's the problem." Her shallow breaths became gasps.

"How is that a problem? It's not supposed to be awkward, Ember."

"This is too easy. It's easy to let go as long as you're touching me." That admission scared her. He saw it in her eyes. And this was why he would never hurt her.

"I like the sound of that. I want you to let go." Fuck. He never had someone depend on him before. Never had an innocent person trusted him. She didn't know the real him, didn't know the horrible things he'd done, would still do when necessary.

"But..."

"No buts." He interrupted her and thrust two fingers inside her. He wasted no time curling them to hit her sweet spot while his thumb drew circles around her clit, wanting to finish where they left off last time.

It registered that they were still in the kitchen. King wasn't sure what he was going to do about that. He didn't see any reason not to give in to temptation and take her right there.

Ember's hips tilted toward him and a whimper escaped from her throat. He applied more pressure and moved his fingers faster. He brushed his lips over hers before whispering against them. "Come." His command spurred a cry, and she tightened around his fingers. She moaned with short breaths while her walls contracted. King continued to stroke her until she lost the ability to hold herself up. "I'm not waiting to get you to the bedroom."

King pulled her pants past her hips and lifted her onto the counter with his hands under her thighs. He tore them the rest of the way off, then pulled at her sweater. "Lift your arms." She did. He had her naked on his kitchen counter and King couldn't wait to devour her.

THE COOL COUNTER shocked her system, but the rest of her heated. Ember felt tiny, caged in, although that was the case with most people. But with King, vulnerability mixed with desire to create something potent. She froze, unable to move, and not sure she wanted to. A smattering of black hair covered his chest, but didn't hide any definition in his torso. She'd had a few opportunities to look her fill, but her head had been more focused on survival. Now, she let her eyes trace the shapes outlined on his chest and abdomen and to trace the different tattoos lining his arms. Ember wanted to reach out and touch him, but she didn't dare, for fear of breaking whatever spell he'd put her under.

"Undo my jeans, Ember."

"I can't." She shook her head once, letting her eyes lift

away from his chest. She considered herself lucky that he looked amused. "I don't dare move."

The unspoken threat in his glare sent a thrill to her core. The big bad wolf threatened her, and she got wetter. King reached for the button, popped it open, and unzipped the fly. His cock jumped free as he pulled them down and kicked them to the side. "Brace yourself, girl."

King looped his arms under her knees, pulling her forward to line up with the edge of the counter. The head of his cock breached her entrance, but he paused.

"Look at me, Ember." She'd been watching every move he made. "Ember." He warned her again, so she lifted her eyes to his. At that moment, she knew he wouldn't be gentle.

He grinned, an evil one, just before he pushed into her. The thickness, the fullness--she couldn't have asked for anything better. He paused only when he reached full hilt. After dragging himself out, he slammed into her and started a hard, rhythmic pace. She'd been right. He wasn't gentle, but Ember accepted every bit.

Her limbs seemed to gather their own courage and her arms wrapped around his shoulders. "That a girl." His low growl sent warmth rushing through her--a small taste of approval from a man like King. One of his hands slid down her leg, taking her foot to hook around him. Then he gripped her breast, kneading it a couple times before lifting it up as a feast for his bent head. He sucked her nipple into his mouth, his teeth nipping around every pull.

"Ah." The sudden sharpness made her yelp. He continued to nip and suck while pounding into her. Everything tightened, and a haze took over her mind. Pleasure radiated through every part of her body. "Please." She begged for nothing and everything.

"Come." The rough growl rolled down her spine.

"No. I don't want this to end," she whined. She'd worry about how she sounded later.

"It's just beginning." Ember searched his face. He was tense, but not in the same pleasurable agony as she. "Come." He commanded her again and Ember stopped fighting it, embracing it wave after wave.

When the last contraction receded, she leaned her head against his shoulder. He still throbbed inside her. Tightening his hands on her hips, King lifted her from the counter and left the kitchen. Ember didn't have enough strength to hold on, but he had her well settled against him.

King put his knees on the bed and leaned forward, following her down, never losing their connection. Pulling her arms from around his neck, he put them above her head. He kept one hand over her wrists. She tried to move them, tried to bring her arms down. His eyes narrowed on hers. His pupils dilated and his jaw tensed. No fear invaded, not with King above her despite the glimpse into his lethal side.

She felt herself dampen around his cock and from the look on his face, so did he. He thrust again, harder and faster than he had in the kitchen. He didn't allow any build up. Pleasure surged as if she hadn't just climaxed.

Her wrists hurt from the pressure he put on them, but she wouldn't say anything to make him stop, assuming he would.

The edge approached, sharp and high, but he pulled out with a growl. His cock lay on her belly. She looked down, expecting to feel hot spurts across her stomach, but he didn't come. "One more."

King eased back inside her and her body, still wrung tight, reacted instantly. Flames lanced from her core, licking at the edge of her climax again.

He pulled out to grip her hips and flip her over. Ember didn't have time to register the emptiness. He squeezed her ass, using his thumbs to open her. She screamed when he slammed into her. The angle full and tight, a little on the painful side, but more than ready to combust, that Ember welcomed the pain with the pleasure.

One of King's hands left her ass. His fingers grazed her clit just before he pinched it. The climax took over and brought her to the end of her ecstasy. King froze for a moment before pulling out and thrusting his cock along her ass, sending his seed onto her lower back.

Ember flopped forward as soon as his hands released her hip. King had left, but returned with a warm cloth. He ran it over her back and between her legs, making her gasp at the terry cloth fabric over her sensitive flesh.

King lay down and tucked her against him, pulling the covers around them. Before she drifted off into what she assumed would be the best sleep she had in a long time, he lifted her chin with his finger. His head came down, and he claimed her mouth in a soul wrenching kiss. When he finished, he tucked her head under his chin. Ember licked her swollen lips and settled against him, her eyes fast closing to chase dreams.

9

Warmth slowly leached away, waking Ember. She stretched her arm toward the other side of the bed and found cold sheets. Her body ached and shivers raced over her. All her control had abandoned her with King. Not because he took it away, but because her own body didn't allow her any. She could control awkward encounters, but with King, it was all so simple.

Shock registered as the sheets continued to cool over her naked skin. With so many uncertainties and the ease she had opening up to King, she should be terrified, not sleeping with the man. She tried to reach for that fear, hoping it would help her pull away from King.

She hated waking alone like this. Hated that he left her again. A convenient unwanted pawn. Was that how King saw her?

Ember breathed deep, storing her strength. She went to the bathroom to have a quick shower before searching through his clothes again for something to put on since they'd left their clothes in the kitchen.

King and Dak sat at the island with coffee and eggs in

front of them. Ember made a beeline for the coffee. As she replaced the carafe, hardness pressed against her back. She tried to tense, but her body betrayed her, melting against King. His breath heated the shell of her ear.

"You okay?"

"Of course." She forced the words out.

"If I had stayed in bed, I would have taken you again." As if he read her mind, he gave her the reassurance she needed. She bit the inside of her lip to keep herself from revealing her uncertainties. Reassured or not, she'd been alone in a stranger's cold bed. King nipped her ear and stepped back. "Breakfast?"

"No, thank you. I'm not hungry."

"Guess I didn't do my job last night."

Her head snapped up. She hadn't meant it as an insult, but King had said it loud enough for Dak to hear. Mortification heated her face as she looked at Dak.

"Don't worry, sweetheart. He didn't tell me anything I didn't already know."

Ember glared at King. He didn't seem like the type to brag--a reserved man who didn't give a shit of other's opinions. "You."

"Careful, Ember." His damn warning again. One of these times she wouldn't give a shit about his consequences.

"King didn't have to say anything. You left your clothes in the kitchen." Dak continued to eat and sip his coffee without a care in the world.

She closed her eyes in humiliation. It was bad enough her body betrayed her, but now she'd made a scene over nothing but insecurities. Ember took her coffee and sauntered out of the kitchen before she made things worse.

"Smooth." Dak dragged out the word.

King glared at him. "You didn't help."

"Not my job to help you with that." Dak grinned, an almost laugh shaking his lips. King had never seen the man laugh. But it only lasted a moment, and he sobered. "What are you doing, King?"

"I've discovered I don't know what I'm doing anymore." King leaned his hands on the island and looked across at Dak. "Was I wrong to retire?"

Dak didn't look at all shocked by the question. "Yes."

"Why didn't you say something? I've never even asked what you've been doing since."

"No one can change your mind but you." He paused before answering the second question. "I didn't want to be in the business alone. The ones that are alone don't last. We've had each other's backs for too long. I've been doing low key jobs while building a security firm. You want to get back into the business?"

King shrugged. "Not with Ember in the picture."

"Is she in the picture?"

"Isn't that an interesting question?" He pushed off the counter. King had no answer for that. He'd never acted this way with a woman. He should have locked her up the moment she arrived. "Any idea what the connection to Bellamy is yet?"

"It has to be there, but I can't find it." Dak pushed his plate away and picked up his coffee.

"I don't want to sit around much longer."

"Agreed. Go after Bellamy in a day or so?"

"No. Today. At least track him down. If you can follow him, good. If you can corner him, great. If you can grab him, then bring him back here. I want answers." King welcomed the adrenaline coursing through his veins. The man might be Ember's father, but any man that would hand over his daughter to a monster wasn't a good father. He didn't care about the reason. It was inexcusable.

"You got it." Dak finished the last drink of his coffee and left.

King wanted to find Ember, but he needed time to think. It surprised him Dak hadn't agreed with his decision to retire. That life no longer held the appeal it once did, but at the moment, something was missing.

Ember sat in the same chair in the living room with the book in hand. Had she been what was missing? A black-haired young innocent?

"Come with me. Bring the book."

She wouldn't meet his eyes, but she rose from the chair and followed him into the study. Coffee in one hand, the book in the other.

"You can read in here." She frowned and turned back toward the living room. "Don't bother questioning me. And Ember?"

She looked up at him, eyes hooded and cautious.

"I didn't intend to embarrass you." He cupped her jaw and ran his thumb over her cheek. She nodded, but still said nothing to him. He let her go, and she settled in a chair, opening the book again.

King kept an eye on her while he worked. He finished with the hotel accounts and checked on Ember. "Ember?" No answer. She leaned toward the book, hunched in the seat. "Ember?" He tried again, but still no answer. Instead of startling her like last time, he left her. In the security office, he called Dak, but it went to voicemail. A few minutes later, Dak called him back.

"You got him?"

"No. He has an escort. I'm not so sure it's a police escort."

"You're kidding." Why would Bellamy have an escort?

"Wish I was. I'm sticking around to see if his company leaves, but I doubt it. Might come back tonight."

"Can you get eyes on them?" If they could identify his escort, they might discover who controlled this.

"Going to try."

"Keep in touch." The call ended without a reply from Dak.

Back in the study, Ember continued to read, but she'd almost reached the end of the book. King sat on his desk and waited for her to finish.

"Holy shit." She breathed as she closed the book. She had a bit of a mouth on her.

"How did it end?" Ember jumped at King's voice. He'd waited until she finished to avoid scaring her and risk getting beaten with a book, but it looked like that didn't matter.

"It was," she paused, looking like she was searching for the right word. "It was messed up. I couldn't have guessed that ending if I'd tried."

"Do you read a lot?"

"Not that often. It's something I have to be in the mood for. Whenever I need a little escape from the stress of life." She got up from the chair and took the book back to the shelf where she found it.

Ember slid the book back between the others, then turned around. She stunned King. Curling her toes into the carpet, she planted her feet next to the shelf. Bare legs reached up until his boxers poked out from his shirt, once again tied at her hip. Her hair draped over both of her shoulders. She was a beautiful woman, inside and out, it seemed. Peaceful, innocent, and a bit of a brat. He liked that. But she was a challenge he didn't know how to deal with.

He lifted a hand and crooked his finger, beckoning her across the room, but she shook her head.

"What are you, were you? What did you do?" She leaned her shoulder against the bookshelf.

"Ember. I've told you. I did bad things."

"Like what?" She tilted her head, never taking her eyes from him. Blatant curiosity replaced her earlier embarrassment.

"Come here." This time, she listened and walked across the room. When she was in his reach, he grabbed her wrist and pulled her between his legs. "Are you sure?"

"Yes."

"There's no going back."

"Please, King?" Her pleading green eyes did him in. She only asked to understand the man she'd slept with.

"I was a mercenary. I did jobs for hire. Not always good ones." He watched for her reaction, but she frowned.

"Such as?" The damn woman wanted examples.

"Everything under the sun, Ember."

"Have you killed anyone?" Her soft curiosity made the question innocent.

"Too many to count."

Her breath hitched, some trepidation showing. Good. King made sure his hands never left her body for this conversation. "Kidnapped?"

"With ease." Now that he gave her answers, he wouldn't mince them.

"You said not always good ones. Were there good jobs?"

"Don't be looking to me for a hero."

"I'm not. I knew you were dangerous the moment I opened my eyes on your couch. I just want to know, King."

"Many times, parents or families of victims would hire me to re-kidnap someone and return them home and sometimes they'd hire me to avenge someone or make sure justice was served. Not society's version of justice." King refused to let her go, not that she tried to get away from him. Her hands rested on his arms and her eyes seemed to see past his. "I have some morals."

"And what are your morals?"

"You ask too many questions." He pulled her a little closer, calm settling over him when she came willingly. She shrugged. "I did nothing to anyone that didn't deserve it and I never involved children, except to return them home. But never forget, the king of mercenaries earned that title for a reason. My morals are a personal secret. No one would leave someone on my doorstep with the expectation, or even the hope, of them being anything less than severely harmed or worse."

She swallowed before whispering, "What about..."

"That's enough questions, little girl." He cut her off. "Do you want to run screaming?"

She shook her head several times. "No. I should. Any sane person would. But I don't want to."

"What do you want?"

A flush ran up her neck to her cheeks. He should make her say it. He set her in front of him, but still within reach. "Take your clothes off."

"King, I'm not sure."

Instead of satiated this morning, she'd been stiff and upset. Embarrassed. He'd thought her embarrassment stemmed from Dak being in the room, but now he wondered if she'd been embarrassed by her actions, of what they'd done. With a firm grip on her chin, King forced her to look at him. "What aren't you sure about?"

"I..." Clear eyes met his despite her lack of words. Her

fingers flexed on his arms and her body leaned forward and back with every breath.

"Your mind will catch up to your body. Now, take off your clothes." King released her chin to give her the chance to obey or run.

She untied the knot in his shirt, then pulled the boxers down over her hips. The T-shirt covered what she'd just revealed. Gathering the hem of the shirt, she pulled it over her head and let it fall behind her.

King stripped from his clothes and grabbed her wrist, pulling her back to him so her breasts pressed against his torso. Lifting her, he walked over to the closest chair and sat down. Slipping a hand between them, he lined his cock up with her cunt and put pressure on her hips to bring her down over the head. No wasting time. He wanted this to be fast. With both hands on her hips, he pulled her down all the way while thrusting his hips upward.

"Ow ow ow." The words came out as quick gasps.

"You're sore. Ride me."

"Oh, I'm okay." She shook her head, thinking he only tried to make it easier on her.

"Ride." One hand slid up her back and into her hair. He twirled the raven waves around his hand until he had a firm grip. He pulled. Just enough to tilt her head. She moaned, one of pleasure rather than pain.

Lifting herself, she lingered over him. King gave her a few minutes to get started. He took her mouth in a hard kiss, sliding his tongue over hers. The grip in her hair gave him the perfect angle.

Ember increased the pace on her own, moaning into his mouth. He met her halfway with his hips, thrusting upward as she came down.

"Harder, Ember." Not a plea, but a demand, a craving for her to do as he told her.

And with a whimper, she did. King moved his other hand from her hips to use his fingers over her clit. His orgasm swelled, rushing to the base of his spine. Moments later, her silken walls squeezed his shaft, and her thrusts turned short and jerky while she came on top of him. King had to clench his teeth to keep from spilling himself inside her. As soon as her orgasm ended, he pulled her off just in time for him to come between them into empty space rather than the inviting heat of her cunt.

Holding her against him, King added another question for himself. Was Ember here to stay?

10

———

Dak stood in the shadows at the side of Bellamy's house. Two cars took turns driving past and sometimes parking. The unpredictable patterns made it difficult for Dak to grab Ember's father. But he could get inside the house.

Dak made his way to the back, where he'd found the loose basement window the last night they'd brought Ember home. Prying it open, he gripped the top and swung himself in feet first. He let his eyes adjust before moving through the dark. When shadowed shapes formed in his sight, Dak found his way to the basement stairs and kept his steps next to the rail. Opening the door enough for him to fit through, he stepped into the kitchen. Street lights shone through the windows.

Silent feet carried Dak through the lower level. It appeared Bellamy had gone to bed. Except Dak saw a faint glow from the back office. Bellamy sat in a chair next to a dying fire with his head bobbing toward sleep.

Shadows were Dak's best friend, and he found the

perfect one at the side of the room. Bellamy shook his head with a snort.

"Where's your daughter, Samuel?" His intimidation echoed across the room. Bellamy straightened, dropping the glass he'd been balancing in his hand. It landed with a thud on the carpet in front of him.

"Who's there?" His head spun around, scanning over Dak, but never seeing him.

"Where's your daughter?"

"I don't know. Someone took her. Who are you?"

"Someone huh?" Dak watched his face for any tell, any sign of guilt.

"Was it you? What did you do with my daughter?"

"We both know it wasn't me." Menace dropped in his voice, telling the man his secret was out. Bellamy squirmed and audibly swallowed.

"I don't know what you're talking about." His rushed defense wouldn't fool a child.

"Why'd you do it, Sam?" Dak had no respect for this kind of man.

"Please. Is she safe?"

Dak laughed low, revealing the savage in his soul. "You know who you gave her to, don't you? What do you think?" He didn't deserve the peace of mind knowing that King hadn't hurt Ember. Bellamy's breathing sharpened, and he clenched his jaw. Agony and anger danced across his features. He moved to stand, but Dak tsked, stopping his progress. "Don't move, Bellamy. That's it. Just sit back down. Now, who's your puppet master?"

"I... Someone kidnapped her." Torture twisted his voice. "Just... Ember..." His phone on the desk rang, cutting him off.

"Let your machine get it."

"I can't." He rose from his chair and walked to his desk. "Samuel Bellamy," he answered.

Dak readied himself to do what he needed if the man did something foolish like turn on a light or reach for a weapon, but he didn't. Bellamy listened, then hung up without saying another word. "Please, don't hurt my daughter any more than you have."

Dak stayed still and silent.

"Hello? Are you still there?" Dak wanted him to think he'd already left. "Hello?" The man slumped down in his chair. "My baby." His head fell into his hands, and Dak watched the man sob. Someone scared Ember's father more than the king of mercenaries. Unless he didn't understand the full nature of King.

Bellamy got himself under control and he left the room. Dak waited, tracking the man's footsteps through the house and up the stairs. The soft thumps ended. Dak left the shadows and went back to the basement to escape out the window.

He put himself in King's shoes, imagining how he would have handled Ember. He wouldn't have taken her to bed, but he wouldn't have returned her either.

THE BRIEF ALARM in the early hours of the morning indicated Dak's return. King rolled Ember off his arm. She never stirred, her breathing consistent and deep. Something clenched at the sight of a woman in his bed. Wherever that bed had been, he'd never allowed a woman in it. Approaching forty years old, he'd been in an aimless fit, retiring long before his time. Aimless because he had no future for himself. His only goal had been to get through each day. Things changed. And Ember wasn't leaving.

He pulled on a pair of sweatpants and met Dak in the hall. They entered the security office without a word, locking the door behind them in case Ember awoke.

"I got inside." Dak dropped into a chair. "Scared him. He tried to play innocent. He doesn't believe his daughter is safe anymore, but I got the impression that was the case whether or not she was here."

"What the hell has that man done?" A rhetorical question, but one King wanted answered. By Bellamy himself.

King went back to bed. The bed dipped and Ember's sleepy moan shot straight to his groin. She rolled toward him as he put his arm around her shoulders. Still asleep, she tangled her legs with his and tucked her face against his chest, settling in with a contented sigh.

Anger toward her father coursed through him, but King doused it until it settling, simmering in his chest. He ticked off all the ways he'd deal with that piece of shit before he'd retired. Bellamy wouldn't be the first man King took out for handing over his innocent daughter to a monster.

One arm wrapped around her shoulders, holding her tight, and one hand resting on her hip, King kissed her head and allowed himself the peace of her bare skin next to his. He needed that peace to forget what kind of man he was.

* * *

EMBER'S NOSE TWITCHED, trying to dislodge whatever tickled it. Coarse hair rubbed over her face and a hard chest vibrated with laughter.

"Good morning." She felt the words more than heard them, his chest rumbling against her.

Stretching, she tilted her head back. A shadow lined his jaw and his mussed hair looked better than when freshly showered. She'd slept with him again. And after he'd revealed his past. Scared? No. Aroused? Yes. What the hell was wrong with her? Every touch and gaze built an unfathomable connection between them.

Foolish. Nothing good would come of this–of sleeping with a deadly mercenary in hiding. She wasn't naïve enough to imagine some happily ever after because he'd retired and was a changed man. She had to consider her own morals.

Some morals. Her leg hooked around him so his cock pressed against her ever-dampening core.

Ember settled her cheek against King's chest, taking it all in now before examining said morals.

The smell of coffee and something else drifted into the bedroom.

"Mmmm."

"Is that sound for me or for the coffee Dak just made?"

"The coffee." She smiled against his chest.

"Huh." His little huff made her giggle. "I suppose we should go get some before Dak drinks the whole pot."

"He couldn't drink that much."

"He could." King smacked her ass. "Up you get, little girl. Before I decide coffee can wait."

She rolled away and stood, pulling the sheet with her. King yanked the fabric out of her grasp.

"Hey!"

"Trying to cover yourself from me?" A lazy smile curved his lips while his eyes grazed down her body.

"No, I suppose not, but my clothing choices are overwhelming." She rolled her head back, emphasizing her sarcasm.

"You're not wearing only a sheet in front of Dak."

"It's more than I wore on my first night here." She planted a fist on her hip.

"Things have changed." His eyes narrowed. She narrowed hers back, but let it go, not wanting to dig into his last statement. Instead, she pulled out another pair of boxers from his dresser. She rolled the waist then found a hoodie that hung on her like a dress.

"Coffee." Ember made a sharp turn on the ball of her foot and left King behind. Dak watched her progress across the living room, his thumb frozen over the remote to the television. Ember kept moving straight to the caffeine calling her name.

She stayed there. Dak wouldn't hurt her, King wouldn't let him, but he still scared her a little.

"King! Ember!" Dak's voice boomed from the other room. It startled her enough her hands shook as she poured, sloshing some of the hot liquid onto her fingers. She wiped the coffee off with King's shirt and went back into the living room. King came in, pulling his shirt over his head.

"You know him?" Dak looked at her and pointed to the TV with the remote in his hand.

Ember almost dropped her coffee. She had to walk to the end table and set the mug down, her eyes never leaving the screen. Jamie was in front of the police station, pleading for help to find Ember.

"She's important to me." He ran his hand over his chin in a gesture to compose himself. "Please. I love her. Ember Bellamy needs to be brought home. Safe." He closed his eyes and stepped back from the microphone.

Both Dak and King stared at her, but Ember glared at her ex on the screen. They'd never been serious. What must King think of her now?

"He's lying."

"That's obvious." King shrugged.

"How did you know?"

"Job hazards. Anyone with eyes can see that as an act."

"We were never serious. I broke it off when I came back for the summer." She tried to state it simply, but she'd glued her hooded glance on King.

"Do you think I care if you have a lover?"

Disappointment pierced Ember in the gut. Of course, he didn't care about a convenient burden. But her damn body refused to listen. She tried to hide her reaction, but he gripped her chin, forcing her to meet his eyes. Ember pulled back, but King gripped tighter.

"A lover won't stop me." His words soothed over the hurt and he released her.

"I don't understand why he's there. We attend the same university. Everything ended with graduation, thank God." She added the last under her breath.

"What was the relationship like?" Dak asked.

"Odd. He was up and down and back and forth. Too eager sometimes. He creeped me out."

"Why didn't you break up with him sooner?"

"I tried, but he always turned it around and changed the issue before I finished breaking it off."

"Flag him." King said to Dak, nodding to the TV.

"Will do." Dak nodded.

"Wait. Flag him? What do you mean?" She asked King.

"He's just someone to watch."

"How? What are you doing? You told me we're only waiting." Her volume rose, realizing King had left her in the dark.

"Yes, waiting," he agreed.

"And what else? Why haven't you told me?"

"That's not your concern, Ember." King changed--a dark leader taking shape in front of her. Ember registered Dak standing to the side with crossed arms. The television screen had gone black.

"Not my concern? I'm being used. And by my father. I need to know. Maybe if you tell me everything, I can help figure out why he would do this. Help you, help my father, help get myself home."

"You want to help your father. It's time to stop being a naïve, spoiled daddy's girl. You've held him on such a high pedestal. You think you can help him, that you can save him from this transgression." King slid his hand along her jaw, invading her space. "Reality check, little girl. Everyone has a monster inside them." Including the man standing in front of her. Ember's hand reared back, and she slapped him. His head didn't budge and her hand stung like a son of a bitch. King's eyes darkened and his height grew.

Dak stepped forward. "Get on out of here, Ember."

Shock registered, and Ember realized what she'd done. A single step back dislodged King's hand from her jaw. The danger coming from King froze her in place.

"Go," Dak snapped.

Ember bolted for the bedroom. Where else could she go? King would find her. At least in here, she had a lock on the door.

She couldn't say she wasn't naïve--something she wanted to change. But she'd never been a spoiled daddy's girl. Her father raised her better than that. He had to. If her mother hadn't died, maybe she would have been a daddy's girl.

Later, she'd regret slapping King, but for now, it felt good.

11

———

"What the fuck did you think I was going to do?" King glared at Dak.

"I'm not sure, but she was terrified, and as amusing as that was, I thought it best to send her away."

"That wasn't your call." King growled with an unwelcome possession. Dak's interference with Ember burned inside him.

Dak didn't flinch. Neither man could win in a fight against the other. They'd only waste energy. They were too equal and knew each other too well.

"What are you trying to say, King?"

"I don't fucking know what I'm trying to say!" King's ears rang as he tried to get a hold of himself.

"You should figure that out." Dak left, but paused at the beginning of the hall. "Are you going to check on Ember, or should I?"

"You." King shook his head. "She fucking slapped me."

"Yeah, she did. That was brave."

"Too brave."

"Not at all." Dak disappeared down the hall. King stalked off to the security office to be alone with his thoughts.

Leaning back in the chair, he rubbed his hands over his face. Ember meant something to him. What the hell was he supposed to do now? The whole situation forced him to rethink his retirement. But he couldn't have it both ways–keep Ember and come out of retirement. King let out a frustrated growl and sat up.

He needed to do something. Turning on the monitors, he started a search on Jamie Chambers--the name he'd seen running across the bottom of the screen moments ago.

Social media channels and a basic background had been quick to find. A list of his family, friends, interests, all in five minutes. King pulled up his school records and finances. The kid needed to grow up.

Deeper background checks were more Dak's specialty, but King managed in a pinch. Jamie Chambers had a reputation that made King's blood pump with satisfying anticipation. Harassment of women, theft from those same women, and allegations of rape where he'd been found innocent.

"You find Chambers?" Dak closed and locked the door behind him.

"Harassment, theft, and rape." King sounded as if a demon had possessed him. The thought of those hands on Ember brought back something inside him King thought he'd wanted gone.

Dak sat in the other chair and turned on another monitor. This kid wasn't likely connected to the situation, but they searched anyway. Dak looked into the school Ember and Chambers attended, and King looked into the family.

"How's Ember?" Dak didn't answer. King would check on her himself soon. But he wanted to know if she asked herself the same question King had replaying through his mind. What would he have done if Dak hadn't stepped in when he did?

EMBER HAD EXPECTED King to follow her down the hall and to his room. Purposeful, heavy, intimidating steps. But Dak had picked the lock and leaned against the closed door with his hands in his pockets. As if he ever looked unassuming. He'd blocked her from getting out, or maybe his intention had been to block King from getting in.

"That was brave, sweetheart."

"Please stop calling me that." The endearment had always bothered Ember, giving people reason to brush her off. "Brave? I would think slapping someone like King would be considered stupid."

"Probably both. Sweetheart." His lips had twitched, urging her to react.

"And would it be brave if I slapped you for calling me sweetheart again?" Dak scared her, but her temper had been simmering at the surface.

"Your hand would never make it to my face."

She'd clenched her fists to quell the shaking and had narrowed her eyes to match his glare.

"You'll do, Ember."

Alone in the room again, Ember paced. Face the music. She had no other option. Opening the bedroom door, she peeked out. She crossed her fingers on both hands as she tiptoed down the hall. No sound or presence came from the living room. Ember listened outside the kitchen. Nothing. They must be in the study or in the office. Rummaging through the cupboards, Ember made a list of what was there. She wasn't hungry, but she needed something to do and a way to stay away from King. Music or cooking had always been her way of relieving stress. King's kitchen would have to do.

As she piled ingredients on the counter, Ember breathed through the never-ending questions. The most important being what would King have done if Dak hadn't stepped in? Ember didn't think she wanted to know. Slapping the king of mercenaries across the face was taking things too far.

KING'S EYES CROSSED, but after finding nothing more than an arrogant father and a mother with a spending addiction, King and Dak had turned their attention toward the university and the classes both Chambers and Ember had attended.

He stretched his neck on his way down the hall in search of Ember, still unsure what to do with her. It had been wrong to call her spoiled. Not everyone needed to live with a rough past. Even he wouldn't be who he was if things had been different. One day with one wrong turn changed everything.

King hit a wall of scents and flavours as he entered the kitchen. Ember scurried around, cooking a far cry from the small soup she'd made the other day. Bending over, she pulled a feast from the oven--a dish loaded with meat and vegetables, all topped with spices and sauce. And on the counter sat something smelling of sweet apples and cinnamon.

"It smells amazing, Ember." He allowed a smidgen of humility.

"I didn't make any of this for you. I made it for myself.

And that dessert is for Dak." She didn't turn around, but she pointed at the sweet dish on the counter. What the hell had Dak said to Ember to deserve an entire dessert for himself?

"Ember." He walked toward her, but she kept working. "Ember, stop." She did with a sigh, but she kept her hands on the island and stayed there, refusing to look him in the eye. He moved in beside her, reaching across and cupping her cheek. "I know you're not spoiled. I shouldn't have said that."

"Was that supposed to be an apology?" She stiffened, trying to move away from his contact.

"Yes." He reached his thumb out to stroke her cheek.

"Have you ever apologized before?"

"Not since I was a child."

"And that's still the case." She pursed her lips, keeping her eyes down.

"I'm sorry," he murmured.

"Thank you." She murmured, leaning her cheek against his palm for only a moment. "But you're still not getting the dessert."

"Damn right." Dak boomed as he walked into the kitchen, hair still damp from a shower. King let Ember go and stepped back.

She passed both of them plates.

"You first." He waited for her to fill her plate and take a seat before he piled his own. The only time he ate like this was when he went to a restaurant and even that didn't compare to what Ember had made in his own kitchen. "Do you cook like this often?" King asked as he took a seat beside her.

"Only when I'm upset. The only way to get decent comfort food is to make it yourself."

"You should upset her more often, King," Dak said

around a mouthful of food. Ember's grin of pleasure from the compliment was sweet with pink cheeks and trying to hold back her smile.

"Maybe I should," he said under his breath. "But you don't live here."

"I'm moving in."

Ember would have to be here long enough for him to upset her again. That would mean keeping her after this was over. He shook his head. Once she was with him, that would be it. There wouldn't be any changing her mind and going back to her old life. It would be too dangerous.

They finished the meal and put their dishes in the sink. Ember reached for the dessert to give to Dak, but King took it from her.

"That isn't for you."

"I know." He handed the dish to Dak over top of the island, his eyes never leaving Ember. "Eat this somewhere else."

The moment registered, and she took a step back. Dak took the dessert and moved around the other side of the island behind Ember.

"Thank you, sweetheart." He planted a chaste kiss on the top of her head. King frowned. Even Dak was getting attached. Dak grabbed a fork and dug into the dessert on his way out of the kitchen.

Ember took another step back. Smart girl.

"Stop.

"No." Another step. King moved quicker. His hand lashed out to grip the back of her neck. Moving his fingers up, he twisted them to wrap her hair around his hand several times. He forced her face back. The pulse jumped at the base of her throat.

He held her there, watching her fear turn to anger and

then to desire. To prove it to her, he moved his free hand along her hip and to the front of the boxers. He grinned as his fingers slid down into wet fold.

"You're not scared of me, are you, little girl?"

Her nostrils flared over her locked jaw. King slowly slid two fingers into her, watching her eyelids flutter with every centimeter gained.

"That's what I thought." King removed his and spun her around by the grip in her hair. He put an arm between her legs and lifted her while pushing her down across the counter. Her feet dangled a foot off the floor.

"What are... What are you going to do?"

A novel form of punishment for him, but he wouldn't tell her that. She shook, but didn't struggle. She feared and trusted him at the same time. Damn, it was beautiful.

King ripped the boxers down until they fell to the floor and moved himself to the side. His grip pinned her to the counter with her cheek against the surface as she faced him.

"King?"

He slapped her ass as an answer. She gasped, her breath gone. A pink print shone when he lifted his hand to bring it down again. Hard. Ember flushed and her hands flattened on the smooth surface, fingers stretching for purchase.

"Ever been spanked before, girl?"

"No," she whispered.

He made it to the count of five, never hitting the same spot twice. She breathed through every one, and by the last her hips pushed back. Glossy eyes looked up at him.

A beautiful contradiction.

King soothed over her red ass until he reached her core. She whimpered, and he shoved his fingers inside her. Juices coated him, making the passage easy.

"Are you going to slap me again?"

"Oh probably," she breathed while trying to move her hips with the thrust of his hand. King removed his hand and wiped his fingers on her ass.

"Careful, girl." He slapped the wetness on her skin. Ember squeaked with the extra sting.

"I think I'm learning."

King made the next five sting enough for tears to slip from her eyes. If he hadn't felt her wetness for himself, he'd worry about hurting her. But she didn't protest and struggle. Her hips met every strike of his hand.

When he finished, he leaned down until her hazy eyes focused on him. "You with me, Ember?"

She nodded against the marble.

"Good." King released his cock from his jeans. He felt like an ass as he still forced her to stay in place with the grip in her hair. Nudging her knees apart, he stood between her legs. The tight angle didn't slow him down. He thrust hard and her heat welcomed him.

Her thighs twitched, and her walls quivered.

"Come for me, pretty girl."

"King?"

"Now," he growled and pinched her clit. Ember erupted. She screamed through her orgasm. Her cunt milked his cock and King intended to pull out, but it was too late. His seed jutted into her body, and he was helpless to stop it. A most primal possession he should regret. Yet it only made his orgasm more intense.

King may have just sealed Ember's fate. He knew he sealed his.

12

———

Ember trembled. Every nerve in her being begged for an explanation. She'd cried and soared, and it made little sense. King pulled her off the counter and cradled her against his chest. Time and space didn't register until hot water droplets stung her sensitive flesh. His rough hands washed her from head to toe, bringing awareness back into her body.

"King?" Ember lifted her head from his chest. His thumb pulled at her bottom lip.

"Yeah, pretty girl?"

"I like that." Her strength returned to her limbs, and she slid her hands over his chest. "I don't understand."

"Understand what?" King pulled her against him with his hands at her waist, then he moved them down her body to squeeze her ass.

Ember gasped. "That. I don't understand how I could feel that way with you... when you..."

He pulled a hand back and spanked her again, but not with the same intensity as in the kitchen. Only with enough force to reignite the sting, to swirl her senses around until she focused back on him. "Your body is in control and not your head. What is your body telling you now?"

"Nothing coherent."

King turned off the water and pulled her from the shower. After being as thorough with the towel as he had with the soap, he tucked Ember into bed.

She must have dozed off, because when she opened her eyes, the clock on the nightstand read eleven. Glancing up, King's alert gaze collided with hers. He hadn't even moved to turn out the light. Ember laid her hand on his chest and rested her chin on the back of it.

"What's your real name?" Her whisper sounded loud in the quiet room. Maybe that had something to do with the question itself.

"You don't give up, do you?"

She gently shook her head. A smile played at his lips.

"Richard Hall."

She stared, waited.

"I suppose you want more."

"Of course." At this point, she'd take whatever information he offered.

"My parents adopted me at two years old and changed my full name. I became Richard Hall. I never asked my parents about my name before that and I've never searched for the information since."

"Where are your parents now?" Ember moved her fingers through the hair on his chest.

"Killed when I was thirteen. Innocent bystanders in a drug related shootout."

"I'm so sorry, King." She lifted her head and reached her hand up to touch his face, running her palm over the stubble on his jaw. Thirteen was such an important age no matter who you were. Her heart broke for the young man he once was, but she kept her tears back. He wouldn't want them and Ember didn't want him to stop talking.

"What happened to you?"

"I ran. I ran, and I hid. Nobody ever found me. I became who I am. It took a long time and a lot of learning, but I was smart. I learned from my mistakes and others. Ten years later, I was the king of the business. I never went by the name Richard Hall since the day my parents were killed."

"What was it like with them?"

"It was perfect," he whispered in a breath. "Get some sleep." He closed his eyes and pulled her down so her head rested on his shoulder again. She sighed, letting go of her questions, and enjoyed the feel of his skin against hers. He traced a pattern over her bare shoulder, lulling her into sleep. Her eyes closed with the thought of what life would be like if she were with King of her own choosing, and his. Would they have even looked at each other? Would he want her here in his bed, or was all this just convenient? He wouldn't have revealed the things he had if she was just a convenience. What did that mean for her future? Now that she knew so much about him. She faced so many unknowns, but no matter how this ended, her life would never be the same.

KING CURSED HIS PERIMETER ALARM. Dak threw open the bedroom door as King jumped from the bed.

"We have company. Moving slowly toward the house," Dak's sharp tone cut away the grogginess. He waited, knowing his job was to take Ember. Ember clasped the sheet to her chest, knuckles white. King grabbed her sweats from the top of his dresser and tossed her the top first. When she had that over her head, he tossed her the bottoms. She pulled them on under the covers and got out of bed.

"Go with Dak. And Ember?" Terrified eyes looked up at him. "You do as he says." She nodded and Dak grabbed her arm, pulling her away. Dak would choose the best hiding place or the best way out.

King strode naked across the hall and searched his cameras. Two dark figures crept toward the house. He waited to see if more would appear from the shadows. Nothing. He shut off the alarms and grabbed pants from the bedroom. Dak appeared in the doorway.

"What are you doing out here?"

"She's fine. Still only two of them?" He followed King into his closet.

"Yes."

"Let's made this quick."

King reached for the latch to open his hidden stash of weapons, but stopped. "Let's have fun with this." His lips stretched, eager to get his hands dirty.

"I'm game." Dak rolled his shoulders and dropped his chin.

They stalked to the living room in time to see the door jiggle. Dak signaled he'd take the back door in the kitchen. Nodding, King settled against the wall beside the door, taking advantage of the darker shadow. He had to give the guy credit. King would never know someone was in his house if it hadn't been for his security system.

The guy lifted his weapon and scanned the room. The moment before his eyes landed on King, King made his move. Lunging forward, he grabbed the end of his gun in a tight grip and slammed his fist in the intruder's face, missing his nose and catching his cheek.

King followed through with his punch and grabbed the

back of the guy's head. Not letting go of the gun, he swung forward while twisting the guy back. He groaned as King twisted his arm painfully. But it didn't snap.

Crashing and groaning came from the kitchen, and someone yelled Dak's name. The intruder in King's grip turned his head. King used the distraction to wrench the gun from the guy's hand and turned it on him.

"Don't hurt him. They're mine." Dak walked into the living room and turned on the light. Blood dripped from the lip of the other intruder while he held the back of his head.

"What do you mean, they're yours?" King didn't lower the gun.

"They work for me." Dak shoved his employee forward to stand next to the other.

"What the fuck are they doing breaking into my house ready to shoot?"

"That's a damn good question."

"An anonymous job came in." The guy brought in by Dak groaned. King lowered the gun, but kept it ready in his hands. "They gave us directions to this address and asked us to rescue a girl. They didn't give us a name, only a description. Look Dak, you had your own thing going on. We didn't want to bother you when this job came in. It seemed simple enough. They said it was urgent and that we shouldn't have trouble. There would be surveillance and only one man."

"You didn't do your own research?" King asked, then looked at Dak. "You employ lazy ass kids?"

"I don't." Dak's voice dropped to a deadly cadence. The two young guys didn't apologize, and neither did they shy away from Dak. King had respect for any man that could meet Dak's wrath head on. Dak stepped to the side and looked at King. "Bellamy?"

He took in the two bleeding men standing firm. "What

were you supposed to do with the girl once you rescued her?"

"Hide her and not tell the client where."

"I scared him with my visit." Dak sighed.

"Why didn't he do this to begin with?" Her father was trying to hide his daughter.

"Cole, Roen, report that you never found her or any trace of her. You also didn't find any residents at this address."

"Understood, boss."

"You'd both be dead right now if I hadn't recognized Roen after throwing him against the wall."

"If you recognized me when you threw me, why the hell did you still punch me?"

"For being stupid. Which you aren't." Dak crossed his arms and dismissed the two with a jerk of his head. King handed the gun back and escorted the two to the door. Dak turned away and headed toward the study.

Damn if King couldn't understand Bellamy's motives.

EMBER HELD HER BREATH. The small hidden space in the study had a bit of dust, but nothing too bad. All the noise had ended a few minutes ago. She wanted to leave the cold walls, but Dak had told her to stay. No sound didn't mean no danger.

Steady thumps moved closer to the hidden wall. Ember braced herself to run.

"Clear." Dak's deep timber sounded before he opened the door. He stepped out of her way so she could exit the thin room. "Are you all right, sweetheart?"

"Yes, thank you."

King stepped into the study and Ember burst, dashing

across the room. She landed against his chest and allowed herself the luxury of holding onto him.

"Who was it?" She asked, looking up at him. King and Dak exchanged frowns over her head. "What? Who was it?" She pulled away from King, feeling the enclosure of the tiny room again.

"Two men. Someone hired them to rescue you." She'd pulled away from King, but King hadn't let her go. He wrapped his hand around her wrist.

"Hired by who?"

"They don't know." King pursed his lips.

"But you do." Ember waited for his denial or his answer, knowing she wouldn't get either. It only hurt her eyes to stare down the unmovable being. When it was clear they intended to leave her in the dark again, she left the study, pausing outside the door.

"There is someone her father is more scared of than you." Dak's low comment halted her rush down the hall. Her father? Did that mean her father tried to have her rescued? But he'd sent her here. Ember shook. Eaves dropping would only give her more questions. She wanted the truth, but she wanted it directly from King. Ember forced herself down the hall before she heard any more.

She stood beside King's bed, lost in her thoughts, when thick, bare arms wrapped around her. Startled, she tried to pull away.

"Easy, girl." King's smooth tone floated past her ear.

"I don't understand." She sighed.

"I know." King turned her in his arms and tucked a stray strand of hair behind her ear. "I need you to let me handle this. Can you do that?" He lifted her chin, making sure her eyes locked onto his.

"Yes, I can do that. But please don't leave me in the dark."

Ember didn't mind letting him handle it. She only wanted to know what he was doing to handle it.

"That a girl." His deep approval sent heat over her skin.

"Now what? More waiting, I suppose." She hid her irritation with sarcasm, but it didn't fool King. He raised his brow.

"You won't like what we have to do next."

13

"We need to kidnap your father." King refused to tell her the night before, insisting she go back to sleep, but he told her now while they lie awake with the morning sun shining in.

"What? *Kidnap* my father?" Ember pushed herself up with her hands braced on his chest. Her hair cascaded down over her shoulder in waves and tickled his stomach.

"He's the only one with the answers."

"But couldn't we just go talk to him instead?" She sat up beside him, crossed her legs, and leaned her elbows on her knees. She looked comfortable here, with him.

"We need him to talk and ensure he tells us the truth."

"Talk? What are you going to do?" Her shoulders straightened, and she lowered her chin. Knowing who he was, King couldn't hide the possibility of hurting her father from Ember.

"I'll do what I have to, Ember." And with those words, Ember's eyes wavered.

"Please." She pleaded softly. Only a plea. The hurt from her father's betrayal still showed in the slump of her shoulders. She didn't argue or try to change his mind. At least he'd be able to explain why her father did this when he'd finished with him.

"I'll try." King pulled her down, so she fell against his chest. He gripped the back of her head and brought her lips to his. He kissed her, firm, hard, slow, while she untangled her legs and flattened herself on top of him. Her body melted and King relaxed into the bed beneath her.

Fuck. What was he going to do with her? Let her go? No. Ember was his. But King's future lay in uncertain terms, and Ember didn't deserve to be part of his world. Hell, maybe she was only enjoying him to pass the time. She had her own life and own world waiting for her. Did King trust her to return to her life with everything she knew of him?

King ended the kiss and stopped the exploration of his hands that had moved with a mind of their own.

"Time to get up. There's work to do today." King let his arms go limp to the sides, freeing her from his grasp. She padded naked to the end of his bed and picked up her sweats from the floor. The moment had an odd domestic feel that only further confused him. He followed her from the bed, wrapping his hand around her upper arm. Her green eyes locked on his lips. He was a fool if he thought he could let her go.

Before he made his move, Ember leaned up on her tiptoes and kissed him. Stunned, he let her explore. Her tongue licked along his bottom lip before dipping inside. Blood surged in his cock. He needed her tongue there. But the damn girl ended the kiss and jumped back, breaking the grip he had on her arm.

"What are you up to, pretty girl?"

She had her bottom lip trapped between her teeth, but her grin pulled it free. She shrugged and backed out of the bedroom. King took several deep breaths, giving her a head start to the kitchen. Damn, that little taste of her cheeky nature was something to hold on to. Most of her time here had been spent with worry or fear. What was she like the rest of the time? King wanted to know, but he may never find out.

She'd asked him not to leave her in the dark. And he wasn't there to keep the dark away, she needed to know who to stay away from.

He followed her to the kitchen and let her finish her breakfast before beginning a conversation that would hurt her. "We need to talk about Jamie Chambers."

"Why?" Ember wrapped her hands around her coffee and pulled her cup closer.

"Did you know he'd been charged with harassment and theft in the past?" King leaned against the counter and crossed his arms to keep from reaching for her.

"No, I didn't." Ember's fingers turned white.

"What about rape? They'd found him innocent both times." King hated telling her.

"Oh, God." Ember paled, and she placed a hand over her stomach. "He was guilty, wasn't he?"

"I can't say."

"But you suspect. I can't believe I never..." She broke off. He filled in the blanks for her.

"Saw it? You knew something was off with him and broke up with him. He would have hid it well." Criminals hid in plain sight every day. He'd made a living using that skill. "Everyone has a monster inside them. Some are scarier than others and some hide them well. The ones that can hide their monsters are the ones to fear the most."

"Like you and Dak." She was right, but he didn't answer her. Ember shivered before taking a steady breath.

EMBER'S STOMACH BURNED. Without saying another word, she pushed her coffee away and left. The only safe space she had here was King's room, his bed. Curling up in the centre, she tucked her knees to her chest.

She should be busy getting ready to start her masters program, back to life, to friends she hadn't spoken to in over a week. The world wouldn't look the same after this. And the thought of Jamie showing up again sent a chill down her spine.

She huffed. Jamie gave her chills, but a man like King made her melt. The worst of the worse. What future did she have with a man capable of things she couldn't imagine? King wasn't thinking about a future with her. Why would she?

Ember wanted a shower, if for no other reason than to relax. She found King and Dak in the office.

She poked her head in the door. "Am I allowed to have a shower?" A map of her father's neighborhood was on the screen.

"Yes. Go ahead." King stood. "Make it a quick one, though." He kissed her--a sweet and powerful gesture, forcing Ember to rethink King's motives. He pulled away and Ember left. Shaking her head, she stripped and left her sweats on King's bed.

With the water hotter than normal, she allowed herself two minutes to soak in the heat before washing. Her muscles softened enough to ease her mind. Despite every-thing, she was safe with King.

Ember dried and dressed, braiding her hair to keep it out of the way, and untangled. She paused outside the closed office door. Shaking her head, she kept walking. She didn't want to know what went into a kidnapping.

There was only one other thing for her to do around here. Cook.

As she turned off all the burners on the stove, finishing the meal, King and Dak walked into the kitchen and flanked her, each only a few feet away.

"Well? Do you have your plan to kidnap my father?" She turned her head from side to side.

"We do." King nodded once.

"That didn't take long."

"It's not our first time, sweetheart." The bastard winked at her. She narrowed her eyes at Dak, either for his casual talk of kidnapping or calling her sweetheart.

"When?" Ember directed her question back at King.

"Tonight. I want answers now before someone else shows up. Dak's talk with him didn't give us enough information."

"He talked to you?" Ember turned on Dak, crowding into his space. "What did he say?" No matter how close she got to him, he didn't budge.

Dak shook his head. "He only asked where you were."

"He knows where the hell I am!" Ember shoved Dak's chest and turned around to face King.

"Easy, girl." King reached for her shoulders, but she swung her arms up and out.

"No. This is all bullshit. My father lied to me and you two won't tell me anything important. I thought I didn't want the details, but I'm sick of being in the dark." Ember seethed, meeting King's gaze.

"Get used to the dark." He reached up to tuck her hair behind her ear.

Ember jerked away from his touch the moment his fingers touched her face. "Fuck you." That had been the wrong thing to say. King's hand moved quick, wrapping around her braid.

"What was that, pretty girl?" He pulled her toward him and tilted her head back.

"Let me go. I want to be alone." Ember's nipples pebbled against his chest and curses sprung to her tongue. But with Dak's presence still behind her, she didn't want a repeat of the night before in front of him. Her body continued to betray her, and she needed out of there before she said something to push King further. She wanted to be angry, not aroused.

King's eyes dropped. Her sweats revealed nothing, but he'd read her reaction. His cock grew against her belly.

Dak cleared his throat behind her. "You two done?"

"No." King loosened his grip, but didn't let go. "You're a bit too brave, little girl."

"You won't hurt me. Will Dak?" She'd never asked what Dak did, but she'd assumed it had been the same as King.

"You're not in good company." Dak's voice rumbled behind her.

Ember spun away from King, surprised when he let go of her hair. "Then why haven't you hurt me?"

"Not my house and not my lap. And I won't hurt someone undeserving of it either. But things would be different if you'd landed in my lap instead of King's. You're too comfortable here. You wouldn't have this freedom. You sure wouldn't be happy."

"You think I'm happy about being here?" The man must be delusional to see any amount of joy on her face over the past week (how many days?).

"Then what the fuck is going through your mind when you're in King's bed?"

"Dak." King snapped. "You're out of line." Said the man who'd just had a death grip on her hair, threatening her for being brave.

"I'm not." Dak shook his head once. "You two fucking makes things a lot more complicated. Or convenient for the other side. Does Ember know what being with you entails? Does she know that she would have to give up her old life? Does she know that she'd never be able to leave you?" Although he spoke to King, Dak's eyes didn't leave Ember. "Does she know that she already knows more about you than anyone, including myself, and that much information about a man like you, a man like me, has consequences?"

Ember held back her shiver--her insides quaking with the effort. "Are you threatening me?" Oh, she didn't want to challenge Dak, but he'd insinuated a situation she hadn't considered.

"I'm not threatening you."

"Sounded like one." Ember's voice caught as fear clawed up beside her anger to suffocate it.

"Dak." King's heat engulfed her back.

"No threat, sweetheart." His eyes softened, and the condescension drifted away. "You two have some shit to figure out before someone gets hurt or killed." Dak gave them each one last look and left the kitchen.

King grasped the back of her neck and spun her around. "He isn't wrong."

"What consequences, King?" Dak had painted a terrifying picture of a trapped woman.

"Can you let go of your life and stand by the king of mercenaries? Remember, I'm the bad guy." He talked of the same permanent situation as Dak. He didn't want that, did he?"

"Were. You retired."

"You're more naïve than you realize, girl."

"Enlighten me." She couldn't keep her mouth shut. According to Dak, knowing too much put her in danger, yet she challenged them both for more information at every turn.

King's fingers tightened around her nape. "I should tell you everything and more so you'll run away scared. But I want my hands on you. I want to taste you, fuck you, feel your cunt wrapped around my cock. I can't do that if you're scared of me."

"You can't scare me." What a lie. Ember trembled from the battle within her.

"I don't have to hurt you to scare you." King moved against her, pinning her to the island.

"Stop treating me like a child."

"You're barely grown up."

"Then why the hell did you ever kiss me, let alone take me to bed?" Her eyes burned.

"I don't know." King growled and gripped her hip as he devoured her mouth. Ember lost it, going wild against him, needing more and her freedom. Helpless, she let go, sinking against his body to let him do as he wished to her. She couldn't walk away from him any more than she could stand beside him.

HOW HAD KING MISSED IT? He'd considered what it'd be like to keep Ember, but he never considered it a possibility. But Dak was right. She was already in too deep. King couldn't let her go, even if he wanted to. And the thought of never touching her again made his skin burn.

His. His to protect from this world. And from him.

King tore his hands from her and shoved against the island. "Get out of here, Ember."

"Why?" Her fingers trailed against his chest as he increased the distance.

"Now." The snap of leather reins sounded in his head as he held tight to his control. She set her palms on the counter and lifted herself up. She sat on the edge and swung her feet.

"No."

"No?" King crowded back into her space and slid his hand around her neck. Squeezing, he showed her what he could do without cutting off her air. "I've warned you before, little girl."

"If you were going to hurt me, you would have done it by now."

His threats meant little to her anymore. Because he wouldn't hurt her. Ever. The thought alone made him sick to his stomach. He never hurt innocents, but he'd never been ill when accidents happened. Even a scratch on her, on his girl, started a rage in his blood.

"King?" Her tone lacked her challenge. Green danced back and forth in her eyes.

"Go." He matched her tone, begging her to obey him this time. He squeezed her throat one more time, then released her and stepped back, out of reach. Ember studied him for a moment. Her scrutiny made him squirm where no other would.

Nodding, she slid off the counter and left the kitchen.

The food she'd made still sat untouched in the pots behind him. He didn't want to eat. King gave Ember a head start before leaving the kitchen as well.

He hid in the study rather than the office. He didn't want

to pass his bedroom where Ember had taken to hiding herself.

Hours passed as the three of them stayed clear of each other, taking turns eating the dinner Ember had made. King had been the last in there and had taken the time to clean up before following Ember to bed.

She had curled herself into a ball on the edge. King didn't sleep, and he didn't disturb her. Not until it was time to leave to get her father.

Rather than burying his face in her neck and slipping his hands over her hips to wake her, King settled his hand on her shoulder. Ember's eyes opened, and she blinked several times to adjust to the dark. King leaned over her, holding her gaze.

"Time to go." He moved out of her way for her to go to the bathroom. She'd gone to bed in her sweats and didn't take long to get ready.

He left her and met Dak in the living room. They'd both dressed all in black--cargo pants, boots, and long-sleeved crew neck shirts. The tension thickened the moment Ember walked into the room. They'd discussed nothing the night before. King couldn't hurt her, but he couldn't let her go. He had his own decisions to worry about and he needed to figure how Ember fit into those decisions.

But now wasn't the time.

"Let's go." King crouched down in front of Ember. "Hop on."

"What?"

"You don't have any shoes. Hop on my back."

"Oh." Ember wrapped her arms around his neck and climbed onto his back with her feet hooked together in front of him. Dak held the door for him and King took Ember to his car to put her in the front seat. "No blindfold this time?"

"No blindfold." Further securing her to his side.

Dak pulled out ahead of them and led the way. The drive was silent. The implication of the previous night and what they were about to do filled the atmosphere. For once, Ember didn't have questions.

They parked in front of an apartment complex with a security firm on the bottom level. Dak owned it all. King pulled Ember from the car and put her on his back again to carry her to the top floor of the building. To Dak's apartment. Once inside, he set her down.

"Stay here. Don't turn on any lights and don't open that door." King had a grip on her chin and pinned her with a glare.

"I won't." She sighed. "King? I hate being useless."

"You aren't useless, Ember." He kissed her, then left her in the dark to do what he did best.

14

———

They took Dak's car to Bellamy's house. King gritted his teeth when they saw patrol cars passing. They watched the car turn the corner. Dak had said their patterns were erratic, so they waited. The car circled the block and slowed again as it passed the house.

They used the shadows to carry them to the back basement window. Swinging inside, King followed Dak through the basement and up the stairs. They checked rooms as they passed and stopped at the front of the house to watch for patrols before making their way to the bedrooms upstairs.

Bellamy slept on his back, the covers twisted around his torso. The disturbance of their presence was enough to stir Bellamy from his restless sleep. He searched the room, but didn't spot them until his eyes adjusted.

"Hello?" His groggy voice carried in the silence.

King saw the exact moment Bellamy made out their shadows in the room.

"Who's there?" He panicked, sitting up and struggling to get the blankets off him. Dak had the syringe ready and stepped closer.

"It's just a nightmare. Go back to sleep." Dak's voice even sent chills down King's spine. The man had a talent.

Bellamy doubled his efforts to stand, but Dak was faster. He stuck the needle in his arm only a second later. He pushed the end down, removed the needle, and stepped back. Bellamy swayed. King lifted his leg and nudged Bellamy in the chest with his foot to collapse him to the bed rather than the floor. Dak passed a length of the rope to King.

Dak lifted the unconscious and bound man over his shoulder.

Calm and clarity ran through King's veins. This had been his life for so long, and he was damn good at it. He'd earned his title. He'd retired to give his soul some peace. But the feel-good drug of the job pumped through him. King was coming out of retirement.

And with Ember to protect.

Eyes out the front, they waited for patrols to circle around twice. He nodded at Dak to make his way to the back door.

"Shit. Dak, wait." Another car sped around the corner and stopped in front of the house. Four men stepped out. They spread themselves out as they approached the house. "We've got company."

"How many?"

"Four."

"Basement." Dak moved away from the back door. King saw his plan form. They'd worked together for too many years. They often used the darkness to their advantage. Bellamy had piles of boxes and totes filling his basement.

At the bottom of the stairs, they moved to the right. Dak dropped Bellamy in the corner and took his place behind the stairs. King situated himself behind a stack of boxes.

The same window King and Dak had used to get in the house opened upward. Black boots swung through the opening.

The man dropped to the cement, bending his knees to cushion his weight. He paused, allowing his eyes to adjust before looking around the basement.

King stared at the man's face. He didn't know the guy's name, but King knew who he worked for. What the fuck were Lewis Boyd's men doing in Bellamy's house? This wouldn't be the first time King and Dak lured Boyd's men into the dark to get them out of their way for a job.

He stalked toward the stairs, setting one foot on the first step. Dak reached between the step and pulled his ankle. King lunged silently from behind the boxes to catch him, wrapping an arm around his neck to cut off his air and a hand over his mouth to keep him quiet.

Only moments passed until he went limp against King. He held on a little longer to ensure he was out, then carried him off to hide him behind boxes.

King nodded at Dak to make the next move.

The beams in the ceiling above them creaked as another crept along the kitchen. Dak tapped against the wood of the stairs with a knuckle. A steady rhythm meant to confuse, to make them question. Is there someone down there? Is it their guy trying to signal?

Dak paused when the steps upstairs stalled. After a slow count to five, he tapped again. And guy number two came down to the basement. As soon as he turned to survey the room, Dak reached out and pulled. King met him with an upward knee, knocking him out. He caught him before he hit the ground and stashed him with the first guy. Dak stalked upstairs in search of the last two.

King waited until he heard two distinct thumps before

pulling Bellamy out and back up the stairs. He met Dak at the back door.

"Another one of Boyd's. The other two guys must be new." Dak had recognized the first guy in the basement as well. What the hell did Boyd want with Bellamy? Another question for the man King had over his shoulder.

"We need to get out of here." With their path clear, they left out the back door, sticking to the shadows around the house. King set Bellamy down while he waited for Dak to get the car and pull up behind the house. They tossed Bellamy in the trunk and drove off.

About a block away, they passed the first vehicle that had patrolled past the house. Did they all belong to Boyd? Shaking it off, they pulled up outside of Dak's.

King retrieved Ember from Dak's apartment and carried her to the passenger side of his car. They took the two vehicles back to his place.

"Well?" Ember hadn't sat still since he'd pulled out onto the road. She'd twisted around to search the back seat. King eyed her with a side glance. Despite Boyd's guys showing up, it couldn't have gone any cleaner. But he wasn't giving Ember details.

They parked side by side in front of King's house. King took Ember from the car and carried her to the house while Dak leaned against his closed door.

"Where's my father?" Ember peered over King's shoulder. Neither of them answered her. "King?" Her worry broke him.

"He's fine." He took her to his room and set her down on the bed. "Stay here."

"What?"

"I mean it, Ember. Do not leave this room."

He hoped Samuel Bellamy would cooperate. Despite

what he said to her, hurting him would hurt Ember, and King didn't want to have to hurt her.

EMBER PACED. King couldn't shut her out of this. That was her father. Sick of being ignorant and helpless, Ember raged at her father for putting her in this situation. She didn't want him hurt, either. They'd always been so close, and he was always the one she'd always counted on. But that was gone now. No matter how much she wanted things to go back to normal, they wouldn't. Could she look him in the eye knowing he'd lied to her and put her here? She wanted to. Ember wanted to face him for the truth. It was the only way she'd get past this.

She reached for the door. What would King do if she left the room? Sharp pain pierced her bottom lip as her hand settled on the knob. Footsteps passed the bedroom. Ember waited until another door shut at the end of the hall before turning the knob and leaving the bedroom. She tiptoed down the hall, preparing to stand outside the closed door. But she didn't hear them until it was too late.

The door swung open and King stepped out, followed by Dak.

"What the hell do you think you're doing?" She took a step beck, but King followed her. She watched him grow as his anger rose. "Answer me." He spoke through his teeth.

"That's my father." No more than a whisper rasped from her dry throat. "I deserve to know why he did this and I deserve to hear it from him, even if I'm not the one asking for the answers. You can't shut me out of this."

"Like hell I can't." He reached for her arm, but she backed up and to the side, avoiding his reach. His eyes narrowed, and he tried again. "Ember." King straightened. "It's your choice how you get back in my room."

"King, please. I need to hear him say it. I swear I will stand in one spot and only listen. Not a sound. Not a move."

The muscles in his jaw ticked. He turned his head over his shoulder. Dak only shrugged like he didn't care what King did.

"If you so much as move from the exact spot I put you or make even the tiniest squeak, I'll hogtie you, gag you, and lock you in a room. Am I clear?" King's voice lowered to a deadly growl, leaving no question he meant every word he said.

"Perfectly." She choked on the anxiety he created. He wouldn't hurt her. Ember repeated it like a mantra in her head.

A groan came from inside the room. King reached for her arm again, and this time Ember didn't evade him. He set her against the wall about four feet from the door. His eyes pinned her in place. Letting her go, he went back into the room.

Dak may have shrugged, uncaring for King's decision, but he sent her a similar glare as King. Ember believed if it'd been up to Dak, he'd already have her tied up and locked away.

Dak followed King into the room, leaving the door open behind him.

Ember flattened her palms against the wall, holding herself in place. Tears surged, and a scream bubbled in her chest. She may still be helpless, but at least she'd no longer be ignorant.

KING STRUGGLED with his decision to allow Ember to listen in. He didn't want any of this touching her more than it already had. Get her answers and get her away from the door.

He kicked Bellamy when he groaned a second time. His head lolled and his eyes fluttered. He should be awake by now. King raised a brow at Dak.

"I may have given him a stronger sedative than what he'd used on his daughter." The vengeful bastard.

"Bellamy!" King snapped. The man's head popped up. He squinted his eyes and he reared back. His hands and feet pulled against the rope.

"Where am I?" he asked, his voice sickly.

"You're smart enough to figure it out." King waited while his position registered. He increased his struggles against the rope. Once Bellamy settled and met King's eyes, he set out to get Ember's answers. "Why did you send me your daughter?"

"You took her." He didn't even try to make his denial convincing.

"Cut the shit. You know what I'll do to you. Answer my questions and this will all be over fast."

"Where is she?" The drugs still pulled at his consciousness. Dak stepped up beside King and they waited while recognition dawned on Bellamy. He was in more danger than he'd thought.

"Why did you kidnap your own daughter and bring her to me, not once, not twice, but three times?"

"I had to. What he would have done to her." Bellamy's words drifted off and he hung his head.

"And what would I do to your daughter?" King let a grin play on his lips for Bellamy's sake. But his insides twisted.

The man bowed his head in shame. "Please tell me. Did you hurt her?"

"Who's after her?"

"You shouldn't have brought me here." His eyes searched the room as panic settled. There was no time for this. "He threatened Ember if I didn't bring her to you." So it had been a setup for King all along.

"His name. Then you can start connecting the dots."

"Murray Alexander. You shouldn't have brought me here. He's tracking me." Bellamy struggled to get himself onto his knees. "He wants you and is using Ember as the prize. Please tell me she isn't here and is somewhere safe."

King looked over at Dak and nodded to the door. "Get rid of her." With menace in his tone, he made Bellamy imagine the worst.

"No!" The man's raged-filled wail poured through tears streaming down his face. He pulled at the ropes. King felt no remorse. Dak left and King pulled a chair over in front of Bellamy.

"Now, you have more to explain. What do you mean he's tracking you?" King leaned forward with his elbows on his knees and clasped his hands together.

"You just..." He stared at the closed door, silent tears running down his face. "No." He shook his head, his jaw set in a stubborn line.

"You don't know that. Besides, who put her in harm's way to begin with? Don't make things worse by refusing to answer me." King watched the man fight with himself, taking several deep breaths. His eyes squeezed shut and his face turned red. Bellamy had nothing left to lose. At least that's what he thought. But despite what King let him believe, he still had Ember. And King would do everything he could to make sure it stayed that way.

"GET RID OF HER." Ember swallowed when she heard King. He sounded distant, dangerous. She hadn't moved. Her fingers still flexed against the wall. Her father screamed and Dak suddenly appeared beside her. She fought tears, a ball forming in her throat to keep herself quiet. Her father had known the danger he put her in. Why not go to the police the moment she was threatened?

Ember stepped toward the door, needing to ask her father how he could do it. But Dak's hand blocked her, holding her against the wall. She froze. He wouldn't hesitate to make good on King's threat. Dak lifted a finger over his lips then pointed to King's bedroom.

She turned and walked away, hearing the hum of King's voice carry behind her. In his room, she swiped at the tears that escaped.

Dak paused before closing them in the room. "Are you all right, sweetheart?"

"No, I'm not." She used her sleeve to wipe away more tears, then turned around.

"I'm sorry." He took a step toward her, but stopped. "Are you going to be good and stay in here this time? Don't make me tie and gag you, Ember. Not when you're like this." He'd do it, but at least he sounded like he'd hate it.

"I'm not going anywhere," she promised. Dak nodded and left, closing the door behind him.

Ember laid down on the bed and allowed herself to cry, just for now. To cry for what she'd lost with her father. She could never look at him the same again, never be able to trust him again. Not when he picked one evil over another rather than protecting her.

She was someone's fucking pawn, someone she didn't

even know. She should run. Run from her father, run from King, and run from whoever this man was. They were busy with her father, giving her a head start. But where? At least here she was hidden. Until King decided what to do with her.

Ember wouldn't be the same person when this was over. She'd never go back to her father's. And normal life wouldn't have the same view.

Murray Alexander. The name only registered now. Her focus has been that he'd knowingly sent her to the king of mercenaries.

Ember stiffened and sat up. She had a professor named Murray Alexander. He'd taught her twice in the past year. Dr. Alexander was a good professor--attentive and helpful. Lots of office hours.

King's voice sounded off in her head, warning her about monsters. How many more had she faced?

15

———

King sliced into Bellamy's thigh. Spittle dripped down his chin as he tried to keep himself quiet. Dak passed King a set of tweezers so he could pull out the tracking device. They needed to get out of here, but moving wouldn't do any good if they took a tracking device with them.

He'd considered leaving Bellamy behind, but Ember would never forgive him if he let her father get killed. King still had more questions. But they'd have to wait.

King didn't recognize the name Murray Alexander, but whoever he was, wanted King dead and used Ember and her father to do it. A fucking contest. The one to take out the king of mercenaries can keep the girl. Bellamy had believed King wouldn't harm Ember and would keep her safe. King didn't know why Bellamy thought that.

He dropped the small device on the floor and crushed it with his heel. "Stitch him up. Then we're getting out of here."

The perimeter alarm pierced his ears.

"Too late." Dak moved toward Bellamy, and King left to get Ember.

She sat up in the middle of his bed, hair damp from a shower. "What's going on? Is it my father?"

"No time. Move."

Red streaked her cheeks, the sight stabbing his chest. But he didn't have time to make her feel better about any of this. He didn't have to pull her from the room. She came to him, waiting behind him while he retrieved his rifle, handgun, several knives, and binoculars from his storage.

Dak came out of the office. "Four men."

King led Ember to the study. The hidden room had the best escape tunnel. King tucked her between the walls and waited for Dak to follow while dragging her father.

"Ember?" He croaked, tripping over his feet as Dak shoved him inside.

"Not a word, Bellamy." Dak followed him in.

King stepped through and shut the door behind them. Dak had tied white scraps around the cut in Bellamy's thigh. The fabric changed colour. With Bellamy watching, King couldn't kiss Ember the way he wanted to. Instead, he sneered at all of them and left down the tunnel that led outside. Ember's stark face melted into his memory.

Emerging into the dark, King set the butt of the gun against his shoulder. He slipped through the shadows and into position. Laying his body in the debris on a small rise, he waited until the men came into view. Spread out and approaching steadily. Raising the binoculars, King studied each face. He cursed as he recognized them one by one. Zax's men. His organization had been low ball competition for King. No competition at all, but that hadn't been how others in the business saw it. They all saw King as someone to beat, someone from which to steal jobs. Zax was just another kingpin in an underworld of jobs for hire. But the four men inching toward King's house were two of his assassins and two of his thugs.

Now, someone had set up a competition to take out the king of mercenaries and organizations were going to come out of the woodwork. King's secrecy and privacy were about to shatter.

One crouched at the front door to pick the lock. Another jogged around to the back of the house. The two assassins stayed back in the shadows, waiting for the thugs to get taken out first. Not a chance. King put one assassin in his sights, then the other, noting the movement he made between sighting each of them. He'd wanted to take out these two for years. One hadn't only killed for money, but for fun, while the other stood behind to watch.

They disappeared into the house and when no sounds emerged, the two assassins stepped forward. King breathed out and pulled the trigger. The first bullet went through his neck, hitting both major arteries. He adjusted, breathed, and shot the second. Same shot. Both assassins bled out on the ground.

King launched through the night to enter the house through a different tunnel than where Dak hid with Ember and her father. He paused, holding his breath. He listened for the positions of the two thugs. There was a reason the assassins sent the heavy-footed guys in first. To draw King out, making it easier for them to take him out. But King was better. He was thug and assassin, and everything in between.

One searched the study, and the other was down the hall toward the bedrooms. King considered his options. Ember was hiding in the study. He didn't give a shit about Bellamy, and Dak could take care of himself, and he'd protect Ember.

But King's chest constricted as he realized how close Ember was to the likes of Zax's thugs.

He shook his head. He had to be smart. Taking out the one in the study would block King in for an easy attack by the other. King waiting on the other side of the wall with a clear view of the door to the study and hidden from the guy opening and closing bedroom doors. When he jiggled the office door, King tapped his foot against the wall--not loud enough to be heard from the study.

With the gun aimed at the study door, King waited. Slow steps brought him down the hall. King reared the gun forward and slammed the butt back against his nose. A resounding crunch and yell brought forth the guy from the study. Quick aim and King hit him in the chest. Blood rushing from his face, the first one charged. King pulled the knife from his side and spun it around his finger. Pointing it forward, he let him run himself on the blade. Letting go of the handle, King reached up and snapped his head to the side.

The other struggled to breathe on the floor, his hand straining to reach for the gun he'd dropped. King stepped over his body and reached down.

"Want to have a talk, or should I just end you now?"

"F... fu... fuck you."

"Fair enough." With a two handed grip, King snapped his neck, putting him into the same permanent sleep as the other three.

PANIC CLAWED at Ember the moment King disappeared. He'd sneered, but Ember caught the heat in his eyes the moment he hesitated toward her. Dak pressed a finger to his lips, glaring at her father. He clutched at a scrap of fabric tied around his thigh. The fabric darkened to match the lack of light in the small room.

"What..." Ember turned on Dak, but his savage glare turned on her.

"Quiet."

"But he's bleeding," Ember rushed to say before Dak cut her off again. Her father inched closer to her.

"Don't move." How Dak made his voice hushed with his deep baritone, she didn't know. Her father tried to straighten, releasing his hold on his thigh. Now he wanted to stand up to a man like Dak and protect her? Fuck that.

Ember inched closer to Dak, trusting him more than she trusted her father. Dak moved with her, taking advantage. He stepped behind her, his breath smoothed over her ear.

"Sorry, sweetheart. Need to use you for a minute." He brought his hand up in front of her and wrapped it around her neck, holding her tight against him. His cheek lifted like a smile against her head. He squeezed enough that genuine shock widened her eyes and parted her lips. Air and blood flow lessened, but he didn't cut them off. Dak moved them closer to her father. "What's it going to be, Bellamy? Want to see what I can do to her before you make your next breath?"

Her father froze, chest heaving and his jaw locked. But after staring down Dak, he stepped back and hung his head to the floor, never meeting Ember's eyes. That stole her breath more than anything Dak could do to her.

"Good boy." Dak cooed. He lessened the pressure around her neck, but didn't let go. He held her against him, keeping her away from her father. She tried to breathe deep, staring at her father, willing him to show some sign that he'd stand up for her.

Time stretched. Her father leaned harder against the

wall and Ember allowed Dak to keep her upright. He stayed tense and alert behind her, his hand still loose around her neck to keep her father in line. In shame. She'd seen the disgust as his gaze moved from Dak to the floor without hitting her.

Dak's head turned. Ember tried to listen, tried to hear what he did. Footsteps. A yell and a gunshot made Ember jump. Dak held her, his thumb moving over her pulse to calm her. But he only focused on the door that led them out into the study. Or so she'd thought, but a blade appeared in front of her, pointing at her stomach. When she felt the sharp edge, Ember looked up. Her father had pushed off the wall, trying to take advantage of Dak's distraction.

"Back in your corner."

She'd had no one threaten her in this way. Ember tried to rationalize the situation. She was in way over her head, if, while still concerned for her safety while being held and threatened by a savage mercenary, she also felt safer with him than with her father in front of her.

The door slid open and Dak turned the knife toward the opening. King stepped back to let them out. Dak passed Ember through, then took hold of her father.

"Zax."

"Dead?"

King nodded and pulled Ember out of the room. She gasped, holding her hands over her mouth as he took her past the bodies in the hall.

"You did that?"

Dark eyes peered down at her. "Yes."

And Dak had held a knife to her stomach and gripped her throat. Yet, she still wanted to climb up King's body to find comfort. He took her to the security office. After shutting the door, his grip tightened. Pain burned under his fingers. Ember thought he was still mad at her, but he pulled hard, slamming her against his chest. His grip released her arm and slid around her waist, while his other hand cradled the back of her head.

Shaking started in her legs and moved up her body to her shoulders.

"I've got you, pretty girl." King soothed her with his hand up and down her back. His heat seeped into her body, and she lifted her head off his chest to look up at him. He ran his thumb over her lips, taking his time to search her face. Ember looked at him and tried to see the man who'd just killed four men. She only saw King.

When he kissed her, she couldn't breathe. He ravaged her mouth, taking all rational thoughts from her. She clutched at his chest. As much as she wanted to beg him to hide it all, she needed to pull away.

"What happened?"

"An assault to kill me and take you."

"I don't understand."

"I'm still trying to get all the information from your father. But there will be more coming."

She shivered and his hands rubbed over her shoulders. Dak came in and took a chair. He looked at Ember and then at King before bringing up the security footage. King turned her face into his chest, hiding her from the screens. Ember struggled.

"You can stay like this with me or you can go back to bed." He held her chin up.

"I want to know."

"You don't need to watch me kill." King's lips tightened. An image of him doing just that flashed through her mind, and she stopped struggling. Ember wasn't ready for that. There was no hiding who he was from herself. But for now, she'd choose to be with him and listen over being alone. Ember nodded and relaxed against him.

"Are we leaving?" The chair Dak sat in rolled on the floor.

"We should, but we aren't. The privacy here is blown, but I've built so many safeguards that we still have the advantage if we stay."

"And them?" Dak could have been discussing someone on the screen, but King's answer sent hot rocks and cubes of ice tumbling together in her stomach.

"Bellamy goes. Ember stays."

"Goes?" Ember tore her head up to look him in the eye. She kept herself turned away from the monitors.

"Away from here. Where he goes and what he does after that is up to him."

"Is he in danger?"

"Yes."

"Then he needs..." Ember stopped herself. He'd thrown her to the deadliest wolves, and she still felt the need to protect him. He was still her father. "He needs to be protected, too. Please."

"I'll put one of my guys on it." Dak suggested and King nodded.

Ember settled against King's chest again. Their voices rumbled as they discussed which escapes and tunnels to use and in what scenarios. They threw out names of possible attackers. All people from King's past, she assumed. She'd learned the four men King had killed belonged to someone named Zax. Two of them had been assassins. If they'd succeeded, King would be dead and Ember would be with them. But wasn't that the type of person King was? An assassin and more?

DAK HAD CALLED in his guys. Four in total. One would take Bellamy and hide him until this was over. King wanted to throw him back in his home and let karma run its course. But he couldn't deny Ember or put her through the pain of losing her father any more than she already had.

"Can I see him before you send him away?"

King didn't want to say yes. He didn't want Ember hurt more by him and he didn't want Bellamy realizing how safe Ember was with him. He started to shake his head, but stopped as he looked at her. She wasn't eager to see him, but she looked lost and confused.

"Please, King?"

"Okay, but not for long." King tucked her behind him. He walked into the room. Dak took up the rear. He didn't feel Ember behind him, so he turned his head over his shoulder. Ember paused in the doorway with her eyes closed. Dak loomed behind her.

"Ember?" Her father croaked from his position on the floor. Dak had stitched him up after the attack, discarding the bloody fabric to replace with a proper bandage beneath the torn pants.

Dak nudged Ember, and she moved across the room, her eyes on King rather than her father. Heat bloomed in his chest. She looked at him for certainty.

"Oh, God, baby. I'm so sorry. Are you okay? What have they done to you?"

"Hi, Dad."

"Ember?" His beady eyes searched his daughter, then looked up at King. "You didn't hurt her?" He took shallow breaths of relief. "But you said..."

"You might not be so grateful when you find out he's

been fucking her." Dak's even voice came from inside the doorway. King continued to glare at Bellamy, lacking any remorse for the man's conclusions. His lips quivered and his shock turned to disgust as he looked at his daughter.

Ember turned away, but with a breath, met her father's gaze head on.

"Ember?"

"Why, Dad? Why didn't you go to the police? You sent me here, closed your eyes and hoped for the best. With *my* safety. With *my* life."

"Can you ever forgive me?"

"You can't answer me?"

"He has wide connections, further than I realized. I didn't know who to trust."

"Who am I?" King stood beside Ember and growled.

"The king of them all." Bellamy whispered.

"Not someone you should trust." He corrected Bellamy.

"I can't do this." Ember took two steps back toward the door. "All I see is someone who didn't try to save me." She strode from the room and Dak followed her. The need to chase after her and be the one to right this wrong for her rode him hard. But there was still more King needed from her father.

"Time to finish connecting the dots. Start with how you found me and how you know who I am."

"My wife died in a car accident, except it wasn't an accident. She'd had a stalker. For years, we didn't know it. And by the time we did, he'd already grown bold. He'd staged the accident that killed her, wanting to be the one to pull her body from the car. When they released him from jail, he started following Ember, but Ember was only a child. I didn't want anything to happen to her. I asked around to some of my unsavory clients. They pointed me to someone who could get the job done, clean and with no trace. I hired you to kill my wife's stalker. But I never told you why I wanted him dead. Your man didn't ask."

King's man was usually himself, but there had been times he spread out the messenger jobs. King hadn't recognized Bellamy, but that had been a long time ago. "How did you find me?"

"I tried to keep track of you by connecting your jobs. I'd lost you a few times for a year or two, but I found you about six months after you retired."

He'd known it wasn't impossible for someone to find him, but Bellamy found him only six months into his retirement. That pissed him off. He'd never been free from that world. There'd been no point to retirement if he couldn't hide. That darkness would always be a part of him. And after the recent events, he welcomed it.

"Murray Alexander is a professor at Ember's school. But he used to go by a different name. Lewis Boyd. He'd been a client of mine." Bellamy shook his head, curling his lip as he spoke. "I'd gone to him when looking for you to kill the stalker. He pieced it together. When he recognized Ember's last name, he sought me out. He threatened Ember. I had to tell him where you were, but he wouldn't let me just give him the location and move on."

"He wanted to play." Boyd had loved games. Street games, war games, anything to make a job interesting. "How long has he been at Ember's school?"

"Three years."

"How long have you known he was there?"

"Two." He turned his head away.

"Two what?" King wasn't going to like his answer.

"Two years."

King's hand wrapped around Bellamy's throat and

pulled him from the floor. His feet scrambled to get purchase beneath him. "You allowed your daughter within reach of a man like Lewis Boyd?" The tone in King's voice hadn't appeared in over two years. Death itself vibrated through his words.

"I didn't think h..." Each word laboured through a croaked breath.

"No, you didn't. You disgusting piece of shit." King dropped Bellamy to the ground before he hurt Ember.

16

───────

Ember threw everything she got her hands on. The pillows off King's bed, the lamp. The porcelain cracked rather than shattered against the wall. Books, drawers, clothes. She shook with unease, not knowing what to do with herself, how to handle any of it. Disgust, dismay, betrayal, loneliness. So much swirled inside her, leaving her overwhelmed.

Dak had tried following her when she left her father, but she ignored him, throwing things toward the door as encouragement to leave. He'd nodded and shut the door, leaving her to sort through this mess on her own.

She sunk to the floor, holding her breath to keep tears away. She would not cry. This was her life, and no one would move her around. If Ember stayed with King, it would be her decision. And if she left him, he couldn't stop her. The last was a lie. He was King. Of course, he could and would stop her if he wanted to.

With trembling hands, she reached out in front of her to refold King's clothes. She'd covered his bedroom floor with almost everything in the room. She created a mess rather than damage.

The bedroom door swung open and King walked in. His gaze took in the room before landing on her, a quivering mass in the centre of the room. Anger shone in his dark eyes.

"I'm sorry. I'll clean it all up."

King reached down and lifted her up with a hand under her arm. "I'm not worried about the mess." He sat down on the bed, pulling her down to straddle his lap. With his hands behind her knees, he tucked her closer so their centres touched. "Are you okay?"

"No."

"Dak's guys will be here soon. If you want to talk to your father again, do it soon. I want him out of my house as soon as possible." Menace dropped in his voice, but Ember focused on his first statement. She'd worry about why he wanted her father gone later.

"I don't want to see him again." Just the thought made her sick. And it wasn't only because of what he'd done. It was because he shouldn't have been the one to do it.

"Good." King gripped her hips.

"Not yet."

"I don't want you near him until this is over and it won't be alone." His hands tightened, and he pulled her closer.

"Why can't I see my father alone?"

"I don't trust him."

Ember didn't anymore either. "What am I going to do when this is over?"

King frowned, and his hand slid up her back to cup her jaw. His words started with a growl, but voices in the hall interrupted him. He lifted her and carried her over the mess until they reached the hall. Dak stood there with another man. Same height, tattoos on his collar and up his neck. Longer hair on the top of his head and a full beard.

"Ready to move him?" Dak asked, gesturing to the room her father was in.

King looked at her. "If you don't want to see him, go back in the bedroom or to the study." They waited for her to move. She should clean up the mess she'd made, but turning around only showed her how much of a mess she felt on the inside. Ember chose the study, excusing herself past them. In the living room, three other men stood around, geared in black, with weapons attached in every convenient place on their bodies. Wide eyed, she rushed into the study.

Looking through the books, she read the spine aloud as she pulled each one free and back in place, thumping it against the shelves to make noise. It had helped until she heard her father's voice rise in the living room.

"What are going to do with me?" King and Dak had said they'd put her father into hiding. But they hadn't departed that plan to her father. "Please, let Ember and me go. I'll send her away and then try to fix this. I'll try to keep them off you."

The distinct sound of a fist connecting with bone silenced everything. Without thinking, Ember charged from the study. Her father lay on the floor, a cut above his eye and a bruise forming on one side of his face. King stood over him, knuckles tight and heaving for air, until he met her gaze. He stepped back.

"Why did you do that?"

"Because he's begging now to do the right thing to keep his own ass safe."

Ember nodded and turned away. King was right. Her

father could have sent her anywhere in the world to keep her safe.

"Ember?" Pained rasping sounded from the floor.

"Why did you send me here?" His previous answer had been because someone threatened her if he didn't. But if he didn't want her harmed, why did he send her to King?

"Get him out of here." King ordered, not giving her father a chance to answer, not that he'd tried, or opened his mouth now as the guy she'd seen in the hall next to Dak pulled him from the house.

Ember eyed King. He knew why.

"King? What aren't you telling me?"

"Let it go, Ember."

"No." The turmoil in her chest mirrored itself in his eyes. He wouldn't let him answer her. "Tell me why."

"You don't need to know. It will only hurt you."

"I'm done with all of this." Ember squared off against King and the other behemoths in the room. "I'm not a stupid little girl to use. Tell me."

"I don't want you in this world."

"Too late, now."

"You shouldn't be here!" His roar echoed off the walls and stung. Ember was speechless. After all he'd said, after all they'd done. He didn't want her. Dak had warned that she'd already known too much. So where did that leave her? Carted off to places unknown by one of these other goons? She'd fight with her last breath.

But she didn't have to.

"You know what to do." King ground at Dak then stormed out of the house.

KING PARKED OUTSIDE of Lowell's bar after hours of driving. A place full of information on seedy people by seedy people. The owner, Jacob Lowell, knew him, but not his name. His face was King's messenger to most.

He found his usual seat with the view of the entire bar. Two young gang member wannabes spread themselves out in the booth. With the mood he was in, King had no trouble terrifying them with a black look. Both boys shrank back.

"Get out of my seat." His low growl was on par with Dak's. They scrambled from the table and King sat down, putting his back to the wall. Piano music rang out over the crowd, followed by a soft voice. A red silk clad woman played on the stage. Seemed Jacob had upgraded with a new piano and a new entertainer. Last time King had been here, Jacob was trying to get rid of an innocent like her that wanted a job. Guess she won.

She won more than that as Jacob emerged from behind the bar to hike up the stage when she finished her song. Jacob pulled her up and against his chest. Well, hell. Even someone like him found a woman.

King had to get out of his house. The moment he did, he panicked about leaving Ember there without him when he didn't know when the next attack would happen. But Dak and his guys were there. She was safe. And King needed space. The rage rising inside him at Ember's father wouldn't end. Who does that to their daughter, then tries to bargain their way out of it. Between that and his growing feelings for Ember--he inwardly shook.

Retirement had never been possible for him. But what was he going to do about Ember? She couldn't leave, and he didn't want to let her go. But she'd be in constant danger. His weakness. This world wouldn't touch her. He hated that she'd seen the dead bodies, knowing he'd been the one to kill them.

Without remorse and with little effort.

He would have killed Bellamy for what he'd done if it wouldn't hurt Ember. But it was King that Ember went to for comfort.

"I'll be damned. I thought you were long gone." Jacob set a whiskey in front of King and took the seat across from him.

"Not dead. Just not around."

"You been out of a job since King retired?"

"Something like that." King lifted his chin at the pianist. "Trying to class the place up?" The silky clad beauty and her piano were the only shiny things in the bar.

"That's Brook. My wife."

"Wife? Congratulations. But you let her work in a place like this?" He'd never allow Ember to step foot in here.

"She didn't give me a choice. She was here trying to get the job the last time you stopped in."

"I remember." He remembered Jacob leading an insistent and innocent young woman back to his office.

"So what brings you back here after all this time?" Jacob leaned forward on the table.

"What do you know of Lewis Boyd's current status? He goes by Murray Alexander." Jacob's seedy bar worked like a gossip mill for the underworld.

"That cocky fucker jumps from university to university teaching as a professor and uses the campus as both hunting grounds and recruiting grounds. His organizations are huge now, but they're filled with kids who don't know what the fuck they've gotten themselves into."

"What's he working in?"

"Everything. Drugs, sex, money, assassinations. You name it."

Jacob told King everything about Boyd--numbers and locations. Boyd had worked in the streets as a kid like King. They'd crossed paths a few times, then more so after the king of mercenaries stole job and after job from the lazy prick. King dragged his name through the mud. Seemed Boyd had remade himself without King knowing.

He and Jacob talked, catching up on other things. It gave King time to calm down and see things from a different perspective. It was a taste of his old life. And as Brook sidled over to Jacob, King tried to imagine Ember doing the same. He couldn't. He might as well paint the target on her back himself. Especially now that this scheme had blown his identity. It might not be widespread just yet, but it would get there. The next time he walked into Lowell's bar, Jacob might not be as friendly after finding out King had lied to him for a couple of decades.

Jacob nodded at King and took Brook to his office. King stayed until they returned and Brook played her next set. She was very talented.

King considered finding somewhere to crash for the night, but he needed to see Ember. He drove through the night to return home. To see his woman. The danger didn't matter. He was keeping her.

EMBER HID in the bedroom after King left. She cleaned up the mess she'd made, but dizziness bombarded her. Like her body spun around in an abyss. Her father betrayed her and King wouldn't answer her. Every way she turned, Ember didn't see a way out. She could never return to her father's, never return to school, and staying with King might be a future she wasn't prepared for. She didn't need to be here.

Ember couldn't be the prize if the prize was lost. No more allowing herself to be a pawn or left in the dark. She needed to break herself away from all of this.

Tossing the clothes in the drawers unfolded, Ember threw everything else on the bed or in the closet. With a deep breath, she reached for the door. Cold froze her in place for only a moment. She'd be leaving King for good. This wasn't the right future for her, but Ember couldn't deny her feelings for King. Shaking her head, she reached for the door. This was for the best.

But she couldn't just run. Ember needed a plan. With four men now guarding the house and property, they'd be harder to sneak past. Let alone the fact she didn't have any socks or shoes. She should wait, but she needed out before King returned. If she was lucky, they wouldn't expect her to run. She hadn't tried yet.

The alarm would go off as soon as she left and Dak and his guys would be on her in minutes. Those minutes needed to be enough of a head start. Despite her head screaming at her for how foolish this plan was, she left the bedroom without analyzing further, ticking off the long list of flaws.

A dark blond head peaked up over the back of the couch. Noise came from the kitchen. Damn it. They'd spread out through the house. Her few minutes' head start was nil now. But there was more than one way out of the house and King had shown them all to her. Did he have alarms attached to the secret exits? Ember was about to find out.

With slow breaths to keep a slow pace, she walked into the study. Dark blond turned his head to watch her walk past. She'd disappeared before Dak introduced any of them, so she had no names of the others. But that wouldn't matter once she got away from here.

Her steps faltered in the study when another of Dak's guys paced the room.

He nodded at her. "Do you need something?"

Quick, think. "I was just coming in here to read."

He waved at the bookshelves. "I'm Roen, by the way."

"Ember. You work for Dak?"

"Yes." Roen leaned against King's desk while Ember searched the shelves. Nerves assaulted her. Sweat broke out on her lower back. She needed to get out of here before King came back. She didn't want to face him and she didn't want to say goodbye.

Ember pulled a book out and took a seat in the chair. She smiled at Roen and pretended to read, hoping he'd feel uncomfortable just watching her and would leave. No such luck. Roen circled the room a few times, poking his head out to the living room to check with the others. There was more than one escape from the house. King's bedroom had one in the floor. If it wasn't so narrow and deep, Ember would have used that one. She wanted out quickly, not get bogged down by darkness. But if Roen didn't give her an opportunity, she'd return to the bedroom.

"Where did he take my father?"

"I don't know. That's the point. No one knows but Gear."

"Oh. Where's Dak?"

"In the office."

She nodded and returned to the book, turning the page. Patience. She just needed to wait him out. Soon, his visits to the guys in the living room became more frequent and a little longer each time. This was it. Ember acted bored with her book and returned it to the shelf, then roamed the room to look for another, landing herself next to the secret exit.

Roen watched her, but then left for a moment. Now or never. Ember opened the door and slid inside, shutting it behind her.

There was no time to adjust to the darkness. She ran her hands along the sides of the tunnel, unsure how long it went or where it came out. They'd only told her it did.

"Fuck." The low curse came from inside the study. She doubled her steps, bursting into the night.

"Ember?" Dak's angry boom bounced off the trees to her left. The front of the house. Footsteps followed behind her from the tunnel and more from the left.

Pulling air into her panicking lungs, she bolted, bracing herself from the pain of twigs, rocks, and roots under her feet. A wide tree wasn't far ahead of her. She skidded to a halt and tucked herself behind it, listening for their approach.

Someone was close. She held her breath.

"Get on the monitors and call me with her position." Dak's voice was only a few feet away. Ember wanted to slap herself. The monitors. King had cameras all over his property. Half a kilometer. She only needed to outrun them and hide for half a kilometer. Dismay hit her hard, knowing this was impossible. But she had to try, anyway.

Even knowing how close Dak was, Ember made a run for it.

"Ember." He snapped. Looking cost her precious time, but she caught his eyes over her shoulder. A lump formed in her throat. He looked deadlier than King. Instinct quickened her pace. She stayed ahead of him. But more thumping feet came from the other directions. No. She needed to get away. Ember pushed herself harder than she ever had in her life.

Her foot caught on a root, twisting her body so gravity

did the job of taking her down. She cried out as she landed on something sharp.

"Damn it, Ember." Dak cursed, but he wasn't right behind her.

Sheer will pushed her from the ground and to keep running. But she didn't make it another two steps before a heavy hand clamped around her arm. She screamed and struggled against his grip. But he pulled back and locked her against his chest.

"That wasn't smart, sweetheart." Dak called her that with both kindness and menace. He spun her, ducked, and lifted her over his shoulder.

Tears burst as pain stung, but she beat on his back. "Let me go! Please! It's better this way. You said so yourself."

"Not what I meant. And not my call." The other two fell in step behind them as Dak took her back to the house. He took her into the room he'd been using while staying here and tossed her on the unmade bed. "Are you hurt?" Not that Dak sounded like he cared.

Ember refused to answer, even as her entire body throbbed the moment he asked.

"You can tell me where you're hurt or I'll strip you and find your injuries myself."

"My right arm and my ankle." Ember's voice cracked.

Dak walked over and pulled up her pant leg to reveal her ankle. "Needs ice, but it's fine." He pulled up her sleeve. Blood soaked the fabric. "You need to take your arm out of your sleeve."

She frowned.

That was enough hesitation for him and he reached to do it himself. He grabbed the cuff of her sleeve and started pulling it off her arm. Not worrying about where his hand was going, he reached under her shirt to pull her arm out of the bottom and pulled that side of her shirt up to her shoulder. Ember didn't have enough time to protest. She used her other hand to ensure the shirt continued to cover her breast.

Dak turned her arm back and forth. "You need stitches. This is deep."

A sliver of hope replaced her quick fear. "Are you taking me to a hospital or clinic?" An easier escape. She wouldn't tell anyone she was being kept against her will by Dak. Ember wouldn't do that to them. She only wanted to get away.

"Not a chance, sweetheart. I can do stitches."

"Not a chance." She mimicked his response.

"Too bad. I told you it wasn't smart to run." Dak left, locking her in. She tried to set her feet on the floor and winced. They stung with the multiple cuts and bruises from running without shoes. Dak returned, carrying a large first aid kit and one of King's shirts.

"Please don't. No stitches."

He sighed and sat down on the bed. "I have numbing cream, sweetheart. I have to." Dak opened the first aid kit and took out a cold pack first to place over her ankle. He cleaned off her arm and cleaned out the cut. When he did, fresh blood oozed.

Ember whimpered. This had been stupid. And now she'd have to face King when he came back.

"Easy, sweetheart." Dak applied the cream on the skin surrounding her cut, then gave her thick gauze to hold over it while they waited for the cream to take effect. He cleaned the cuts on her feet and covered them with an ointment. The skin on his hands was rough, but his touch was gentle. And Ember filled with guilt for trying to run. Dak didn't have to take care of her like this. He could have locked her in here without another word.

He pulled the gauze away. "Close your eyes." She did. It took a moment until she heard him rustling through the first aid kit again. "You're going to feel me pulling."

Her eyes snapped open, and he had the needle threaded and waiting over her arm.

"Eyes. Close them."

"Have you ever done this before?" Ember couldn't take her eyes from the needle hovering over her arm.

"Lots of times." He didn't move.

"Are you any good?" She wasn't so superficial that she cared about a scar, but that was a big cut.

"Excellent. Now close your eyes, sweetheart." His deep voice gentled, and she obeyed.

Her skin pinched and pulled, but no pain.

"I get that you're scared." He whispered as he pulled again on her arm.

"Why was King so angry?"

"I think you scare him."

Ember scoffed.

"All done."

She opened her eyes to see him cleaning the blood off her arm.

"That's going to hurt when the numbing cream wears off. I'll bring you some painkillers in an hour."

"Thank you."

"I'm locking you in here. Don't run again, Ember. You won't make it." All kindness fled and the deadly mercenary stood in front of her. He cleaned up the first aid kit and tossed King's shirt on her lap.

She changed her shirt, throwing her sweatshirt in the small trash can beside the bed. She hadn't wanted to face King to say goodbye. Now she had to face him after she'd tried to run away from him.

17

King walked into his house and saw Cole on the couch. Roen poked his head in from the study and Hendrick from the kitchen. They all disappeared as Dak entered from the hall. A silent storm.

"Where the fuck did you go?" He couldn't blame Dak for being pissed.

"Lowell's." King hadn't meant to go there or go that far. Instinct of his old life had pulled him in that direction.

"Lowell's?"

"Got more information on Boyd." At least the trip had been justified.

"Is that why you went?" Dak crossed his arms over his chest, seeing more of King than was comfortable.

"I needed a reminder." A reminder of what he'd given up, and that it had been the right choice. It hadn't. He wanted that life back, and he wanted Ember. Two things that didn't mix.

"Well, I had to deal with your captive while you were gone."

"My captive?" Did someone else show up?

"Ember." Dak dropped his chin and sighed.

King frowned.

"She ran after you left. Out the tunnel in the study. She tried to outrun us through the woods. I locked her in my room."

"She ran?" Disappointment and fury warred within him. She ran from him. Here he was thinking about keeping her, and she wanted to get away.

"What did Jacob have to say?"

King inwardly shook himself, but it was no use. "Boyd uses universities as hunting grounds and recruiting grounds. He's grown, but it's full of kids." King spoke as his feet took him toward the hall.

"You should leave her be."

"No." King left Dak behind. He needed to see for himself what Ember felt. Unlocking the door, he eased it open, not wanting to scare her again. She slept on the edge of the bed. Dark circles graced her eyes and her cheeks were red. Her right arm rested over her abdomen, wrapped in a bandage, and she was wearing one of his T-shirts. An ice pack had fallen off her foot and lay beside her on the bed.

He scooped her up, cradling her against his chest. She stirred against him.

"King?"

He took her to his bedroom and laid her down. "I gave you too much freedom. I warned you not to run."

Ember sat up, wincing as she did, and tucked her knees up to her chest.

"Why? Why did you run?" He needed that answer more than anything.

"I didn't want to say goodbye to you."

"What makes you think you're going to say goodbye to me?" He never wanted to say goodbye.

"I saw an opportunity. A shitty one, but it was the best I had. If I'm not here, I can't be a pawn. I have nowhere to go. Nowhere I'm important. You won't tell me everything and I'm done with it. I don't want to be somewhere I'm not valued."

"I was angry. But now I'm furious. You promised me you wouldn't try to leave." His most valued possession. And that was the heart of it. She was his. He felt like falling to his knees from her running away. Ember wasn't going anywhere. King would never be on his knees.

"What are you saying?" Ember tilted her head.

"I don't want to let you go."

"You'll think differently when this is all over. Right now, I'm just convenient."

King lost it. Never had he dallied with convenience. He slid his hand around her throat, pushing her back against the headboard. "I don't say things I don't mean. If I intended to get rid of you, I would have done it already. If I had intended to fuck you and send you on your way, that is what I would have done. I didn't have to keep you here. But here, with me, is where you're safe."

"If you're only keeping me here because it's safe, why fuck me at all?"

"You're not listening. I'm not letting you go." King ground each word out. He hated hearing her talk so crudely. It was fine if he did it, but for her to reduce their time to just a fuck pissed him off.

"Tell me everything." Her voice was clear despite the grip he had on her throat.

"You first. What's under the bandage?" King nodded at

her arm that had slipped from around her knees to cradle against her chest.

"I fell. On something sharp."

King let go of her throat and took her arm from her chest, and started unwrapping the bandage. His eyes bulged as he recognized Dak's handiwork with stitches. "You needed stitches." He choked on his own air so he didn't bellow.

"Yeah."

"Where else are you hurt?" King didn't want to know. But he had to. He had to find out what was worth running from him.

"Twisted my ankle. It's fine. And my feet. They're scratched up a bit."

"Ember." He forced his voice low and erased the anger that was simmered. "Do you want me?"

"Want you?"

He cupped her cheek and ran his thumb over her lips. "Do you want me?"

Her lips parted and her breath shook as she sucked it in. Wide, dilating pupils searched his face. King knew her answer.

"Why run from me?"

"I told you. I didn't want to say goodbye."

"Then don't."

"But there's more than sex. What is there here when this is all over?"

"We'll have to find out when we get there. But you aren't leaving."

King waited for her to protest. To scream at him he couldn't do that. But she didn't. King pulled her lip from between her teeth. The need to cement his claim hit him in the gut. Hooking his hand under her knees, he pulled her to the edge of the bed.

He reached for her shirt and lifted, easing it off her arm that he'd re-bandaged. Reaching for her elbows to lift her up, Ember moved away from his grip and her tiny hands reached for the button on his jeans.

"Ember?"

"I need to." She looked up at him rather than at what she was doing. "Yes, I still want you, King" She pulled his jeans down his hips, enough to release him. Her eyes left his face and landed on him in front of her. Her tongue wet her lips as she seemed nervous to move forward. He itched to cup the back of her head and slip into her mouth.

"Fuck," he cursed. It spurred her into action. Leaning forward, she took the head into her mouth. Wet and warm, Ember moved her tongue from side to side. Too damned slow, she took him deeper while still sliding her tongue along the underside. King focused on the soft heat of her mouth, the light scraping of her teeth, the suction she created around him. His cock swelled and King tightened his hands into fists to keep from burying them in her hair.

"Finish what you want to do, pretty girl." If he touched her, it would be the end of playing.

She pulled off of him and licked her lips like a mischievous kitten. But he wasn't done. Far from it. She'd let the monster loose. He allowed himself to sink his hand into her black silk and pulled her head back so her face angled upward.

"Deep breath and open up."

Realization dawned in her glazing eyes. And she obeyed. That trust was precious.

King thrust in until he hit the back of her throat. Each time, he pushed a little further, so his cock reached deeper.

He kept his pace, satisfied as her eyes watered. She didn't struggle, only relaxed in his hold. His balls tightened, signaling a quick and vicious orgasm.

With a roar, he pulled from her mouth. He tossed her back on the bed and pulled her sweatpants free before undressing himself. Covering her mouth, he devoured every breath she tried to catch.

He needed her. He was in so much turmoil with Ember at the centre. Sinking into her heat, he drank in her moans. Grinding down on her clit to bring her to a quick orgasm, King pounded hard, never getting enough.

As soon as her cries increased and they carried his name, King let go. He pulled from her heat with a guttural growl he didn't recognize as himself. He tried to focus, tried to return to reality, but he had only two words that repeated themselves.

My Ember.

EMBER FEIGNED SLEEP. She lay on King's chest, listening to his heartbeat. She'd had no good reason to run, other than she panicked. A flimsy moment disguised as an opportunity tricked her. She didn't want to face the darkness. And that's what King was. Darkness. But he was also her safety, her light, her truth.

"King?" If she was going to accept his claim, then she needed him to tell her everything.

"What is it, little girl?" His hand stroked over her head, his fingers combing through her hair.

"Tell me." Everything--she wanted to know everything. But for now, she needed what he wouldn't tell her before he left.

He took a deep breath, raising her head with the lift of his chest. "Your mother's car accident wasn't an accident."

"What?" She shoved off him, but he pulled her back down with a hand on the back of her neck.

"Easy, girl. Let me finish."

Ember didn't relax. She flattened her hand against his stomach, ready to move away from him. How was King connected to her mother? He said he didn't hurt innocent people when he could help it. Dark dread coiled around her stomach.

"Your mother had a stalker. The stalker caused the accident."

Ember let out a breath. It wasn't King, but then the rest of his words registered. Acid burned in her core. "A stalker? He never told me that."

"When they released the stalker from prison, he started stalking you."

Her chest constricted and when she pushed off him this time, King let her go. "How old was I?" She'd had a stalker. Breathing created a sharp pain.

"You were still a child." King sat up with her, resting his hands on her knees. His touch should have grounded her. "Your father hired me to take out the stalker. He didn't tell me why I was taking him out. And I only look deep enough to make sure they deserve it."

Her father had refused to talk of her mother's death for years--being the only thing he'd ever kept from her. That had changed. But now, Ember understood why he wouldn't talk about it. He'd taken out a hit on his wife's killer. "So there was a connection to him all along."

"Yes. What do you know about your professor, Murray Alexander?"

"I heard him say the name. I didn't put it together with

my professor until after. But it's a common enough name." Of course, there was more.

"Which is why he chose it. His real name is Lewis Boyd. He's using a fake identity and credentials at universities. He recognized your surname and sought your father, threatening you. Boyd was one of the people your father questioned about me when he went looking for someone to hire for the hit on the stalker."

"He's a good professor." Confusion swamped her, and she had to play devil's advocate. She needed to for her sanity. The sharp stabs of her breathing, the acid in her stomach--all of it increased. The intensity was overwhelming.

"It's an act. Remember what I've told you."

She remembered his warning. Words Ember would never forget. "That can't be true so often. What are the odds I've come across that many people hiding their monster?"

"High."

Everything blew up inside her. "I'm going to be sick."

King jumped into action, lifting her from the bed and into the bathroom. Her stomach revolted, but nothing came up.

"I'm sorry."

"Easy, pretty girl. I've got you." He held her hair and rubbed her back.

"Why didn't he send me somewhere else?" Despite that nothing came up, Ember still felt the need to brush her teeth while she listened to King's answer.

"He'd done his research on me and kept track of me following the hit. He knew I sometimes took the good jobs. Your father took a gamble, thinking you'd be safer with me."

Ember mulled over that while she finished. A gamble. A pawn. A convenience. An inconvenience. She was supposed to be his daughter. But with King, she'd discovered more truths. They may have been ugly, but she was no longer ignorant. Turning off the water, she spun around to face King rather than look at him through the mirror. "Was he right?"

"He was right, but he shouldn't have taken that gamble. I'm furious that any father would send their daughter to me, then try to save their own ass by promising to do the right thing once he feels his life is on the line."

"He's not a bad person. He hasn't been a bad father." Those words were hard to say. But he was still her father, and she didn't want to forget the good years they'd had.

"Maybe not. But that's changed."

Everything had changed.

"You can't run." King cupped her chin, tilting her head back.

And she wouldn't try. When this was over, she'd need to decide and hope that if she left, King would let her go.

King ran his thumb over her lips, then bent his head. He kissed her, slow and deep, then pulled her back into the bedroom to get dressed. Stepping aside, he let her out of the bedroom first. They met everyone else in the kitchen.

"Listen up. Ember goes nowhere alone."

Her eyes bugged away from the geared up men eating lunch and drinking coffee.

"Sorry, little girl. You've lost your freedom privileges." He directed himself back to the others. "I mean nowhere."

Nowhere? Surely she'd be able to go to the bathroom or shower on her own. Ember tried to find even a little sympathy from the others in the room, but there was nothing. Hard edged faces stared back at her. She'd done it to herself, but what would any of them had done in her position? They wouldn't just sit around and wait for others to deal with their problems for them. But that's what they all expected her to do.

"We prepare for more attacks. We could leave, but this is my territory. And it gives us the advantage. Whoever is with Ember at the moment of an attack, that is who puts her in hiding. You hide with her and protect her unless you're needed in the fight."

Ember didn't bother protesting. She listened to them talk while weaving through them to get her own coffee.

"We're dealing with Lewis Boyd. Do you all know who he is?"

"They do now," said Dak.

Dak had changed his clothes since first arriving. He now wore the same black fatigues as the others. Even King had put them on when dressing this morning. Black T-shirts and weapons covered their torsos. Ember glanced down at her sweatpants and King's shirt that she wore. She didn't have to hide her presence here anymore.

Leaning against the counter, she crossed her feet in front of her and held her cup with two hands. "Where's my uniform?"

She received five almost identical frowns. Ember pointed her finger up and down each of them.

"We'll discuss it later." King turned his attention back to the others.

Ember needed to leave before she lost her temper. Being belittled in the conversation was where she drew the line. Pushing off the counter, she walked past all of them until she reached King. His hand across her stomach stopped her.

"You don't go anywhere without someone, and we aren't done in here."

"I'm done being treated like something smaller than a man's dick." Ember tilted her coffee forward, pouring it down the front of King. He hissed at the hot liquid, but his eyes didn't leave her while he used both hands to pull his shirt away from his body. She walked out of the room, leaving it up to them to either let her go or follow.

They had chemistry as hot as that coffee, but beyond that, Ember wasn't sure how she could stay with him. But would he let her go if she wanted?

HE DIDN'T STORM. He didn't growl. But King stepped out of the kitchen on Ember's heels. His pants and shirt clung to him, but the burning lessened to intense heat. Ember had every right to feel the way she did, but she needed to do as she was told and let King handle this. He reached out for her as she rounded the corner down the hall, coming up short.

The alarm screamed, several sensors and cameras triggered at once. Ember appeared around the corner again and the rest ran out from the kitchen, rushing to positions. But it was too late. Trucks sped up the gravel road and off-road vehicles charged in between the trees. They were attacking fast and in numbers. No stealth, no grace. Quick and dirty, with no concern for consequences for themselves.

"Hide, now." King held himself in place to keep from going with her. Attackers got out of vehicles in twos, outnumbering them.

Ember shook, her eyes looking out the front of the house.

"Don't take a tunnel." They could come in from any direction.

Her eyes met his, and her demeanor softened as she looked down at his wet shirt and pants. "I'm sorry." The door bursting open drowned out her whisper. She ran down the hall.

King charged, hesitating for only a second. They were all young. Ember's age. These had to be Boyd's university recruits. Fuck. These kids still had a chance to turn themselves around. He couldn't kill them unless forced to. This would take longer.

Roen was ready to fight beside him. The other three dispersed. Dak and Cole out back and Hendrick out the tunnel in the study. King watched Roen dispatch the first two that came through the door. Swift and efficient, and the two laid in a pile unconscious. The moves looked familiar, and he recognized them as Dak's. He'd trained his guys well. King didn't have to worry with them at his back.

The next kid charged through the door. His hesitation thickened when his eyes bulged at the sight of King.

"Whatever he's paying you, whatever he's offered you, isn't worth your life, kid." A chance and a threat rolled together into one deadly hum. King waited for him to decide. Attack or run. He attacked, but didn't commit to his decision as his movements stuttered. King shook his head and swung an easy punch to the temple, knocking him out. He tossed the unconscious kid out of the way as two more charged inside with battle cries. King wanted to roll his eyes at the dramatics, but didn't have time as he swung around into a roll to avoid getting shot.

Fuck. He needed to get the guns out of the house. King didn't know which hiding place Ember chose.

Slipping a knife from his thigh, King rolled up onto a knee and threw it. The knife lodged in the guy's chest. Damn it. But he wouldn't be able to keep them all alive. Only the ones with a modicum of sense and self-preservation.

Roen had his hands full of knives up against the other guy. Instinctual dread hardened his lungs. Something wasn't right. There were too many of them. King needed to find Ember. He should have hidden with her despite the numbers. They should have left when they'd had the chance. King had never expected a rushed attack with numbers. No one worked that way. Even Boyd had been smarter than this once. But with high numbers of dispensable employees and a sea from which to recruit more, it seemed he didn't care. If he ever attacked like this in the city, a lot of innocent people would get caught in the crossfires. Boyd needed to be stopped.

King pushed up from his knee and turned to go find Ember. Roen could handle whoever came through the door next. But a body slammed against his back, a knife wrapped around in front of him. King caught the arm before the guy sliced at his neck, but the knife swiped down his shoulder. He rumbled with the pain and flipped his attacker over his shoulder, bringing his arm up straight to hyper-extend the elbow and take the knife. With a foot on his ribs, King pulled and twisted until the sickening, but satisfying, sound of his shoulder displacing popped, cutting off the air he needed to cry out.

Tossing him with the other incapacitated attackers, King looked back at the hall. Another two charged through the front. Where the hell were they all coming from? He gained two steps toward the hall to find Ember with every attacker, but he never reached the hall.

His old self, the deadliest mercenary, climbed and clawed its way up his core. The coffee had dried, but now blood soaked his clothes, dripping from cuts and shallow stab wounds. He was done taking it easy on the impressionable university kids. They'd made their bed.

Getting rid of the next one was little less than a swipe of his arm. Sure strides took him toward the hall, but two men, older than the others, charged from that direction. How had they gotten down the hall?

Ember!

18

Ember wasn't sure if she made it into the attic crawl space in time before someone saw her. She'd pulled the door up, then flattened out in the darkest corner.

Ember hardened herself against the sounds echoing through the house. Eyes wide, she glued them to the opening to the crawl space. The space was flat and empty. Despite being hidden, Ember felt exposed. The all-powerful King hadn't thought to put a hiding space inside a hiding space. Right now, she'd even take a box to slip in front of her. If anyone found the door and poked their head up, they'd see her.

A gunshot snapped below her and her body flinched. She breathed through every thunk, metallic clang, and sickening crunch. She tried to imagine herself down there, fighting alongside King. Is that what Ember wanted? Not only stand by side figuratively, but literally? Before all of this, Ember would have labeled herself incapable of being part of anything illegal. But she had a new and cynical view of the world now. King wasn't the bad guy. Not exactly.

Ember covered her mouth as she heard a distinct roar.

King. The sounds increased, quicker, harsher. But none of it gave away the winner. There had been so many that had arrived at the front, and it seemed like they couldn't get ahead down there. If she wasn't so damn helpless, she could be there. Instead of hiding in a dark corner, waiting for it to be over. This didn't do her any good, and she vowed to herself to never be like this again. Gone was her naivete and ignorance. King may have held back on information, but he'd eventually told her all and he hadn't lied to her.

Seems the bad guy that does very bad things is the person she can trust.

Wood scraped. Ember held her breath. The fighting raged on below her and someone had found the entrance to the crawl space. She had nowhere to go, no way to hide herself further.

Light shone inside and a blond head poked up.

"Ember?" A gentled tone called for her.

Jaimie? That sick asshole.

"Ember? Are you here?" He sounded frantic, like he cared. But Ember knew better now. "Ember, there you are." His eyes locked on her with a moment of glee before the mask to match his concerned tone fell into place. "I'm so glad I found you. I'm going to get you out of here."

Ember shrunk back in the corner. Jaimie hesitated.

"Come on, baby."

She cringed. She hated being called baby, especially from this condescending croon.

"Come with me. Your father sent me to take you home."

"Bullshit." That was thick and rich.

"Ember, I know you're scared, but you have to come with me." Jaimie climbed into the crawl space. Ember had nothing. No weapon, no shield, not even long nails to use as claws.

"My father didn't send you. And I'm not going with you." Fear shook her, but she kept it out of her voice. *Oh, King. Where are you?*

"We have to hurry. Let's go." His concern shattered and urgency took its place. He scrambled closer. Ember twisted herself around. If she had no weapon from her hands, the least she could do was kick. "Fuck," he cursed.

Ember tried to see where she aimed as she lifted her knee until it hit the top of the crawl space. Jaimie's hands were out, moving up and down to get a grip on her ankles. She aimed. And fired. With her heel stuck out, she landed the kick right in his eye. Damn it. She was aiming for his nose. But he still cried out in satisfying pain. Good. The disgusting bastard.

"Get up here. I need some help with her." With one eye squeezed shut, he tried again to grab her foot. Another scrambled into the crawl space and hurried forward like a black ground beetle. She wasn't going without a fight. Ember reared back, aimed for his other eye, and kicked again. But she missed and landed her foot in the hands of the other guy.

Adrenaline zinged through her blood. She kicked hard and fast with her other foot, not aiming, and not slowing down.

"Let go of me!"

Jaimie snatched his hand down and got hold of her other foot. They started pulled and scooting backward.

"He's going to kill you." Ember thought the warning was only fair, especially if it made him think twice about taking her. She tried to drag up some sympathy, but had nothing.

"Who? King? He can't kill me if he's dead." They kept pulling. Ember struggled, her arms outstretched, reaching for nothing to hold her back. Tears welled, but she wouldn't let them free. Not now. Not in front of Jaimie. Not in front of anyone again.

Near the exit, they switched grips, so Jaimie was the only one holding her and the other guy slid out. Jaimie pulled her as he followed. The edge scraped against her back. She hissed and whimpered, then fell into Jaimie's arms. He twisted her around, so her back was to him. The hall was empty, but the sounds she'd heard from above were loud and stark coming from the living room. Someone threw a body against the wall next to the study, but he bounced back up and attacked again.

"Let's get out of here." A guy who looked younger than Ember stood behind Jaimie. There were two others with him, too.

Jaimie pulled her backward with an arm around her waist. Her toes dragged on the floor, and she tried to shove his arm free with her hands. When she realized she wouldn't get free, she screamed. She'd meant to call for help, but it was full of emotion instead. The adrenaline and fear, the regret and helplessness. She cried out for King.

A hand slapped hard over her mouth, cutting her off.

"Shut up." He growled in her ear.

But a vicious sound from the living room echoed his growl. King. He'd heard her.

"Move now." Jaimie shoved past the others and they crowded after him as they took her into King's bedroom. Why would they bring her in here? But then one of them lifted the hatch in the floor. How the hell had they found the escape tunnels? Even knowing where they were, Ember had difficulty pointing them out.

Ember struggled against Jaimie with all she had. But they passed no one. He kept a tight hold on her mouth, blocking her air from her nose as he dragged her through the trees and away from King's house. When they drove away and no one followed, she lost her fight.

Someone was going to die. They'd touched her. Ember's scream crystallized his bones as it shivered down his body. The distinct cut off said not only had they touched her, but they had her. King fought with the skill and determination he had when completing an assassination. Concise and efficient, he dealt with the kids left in front of him. It seemed Roen behind him fed off his energy and the energy from Ember's scream to hurry along with dispatching the attackers in front of him.

They all dropped, and Dak and the other two trickled in.

King surged down the hall. They had left the hatch to the crawl space open and the hatch in his bedroom floor. Knowing he wouldn't find her didn't stop him from looking inside and then following the tunnel out.

Back in the living room, he took in the bleeding and groaning bodies. "How many dead?"

"Eight." Hendrick answered. He tossed another unconscious form in the corner.

"Gather whoever is left in here." They needed to make this quick. King vibrated as he looked at the disaster. He'd expected nothing like this.

"Already on it. King, you need to see this." Dak grabbed his arm to turn him back to the hall.

"Ember's gone." He was going after her.

"But do you know who took her?"

King frowned. Dak led him into the security office and tapped a few buttons on the keyboard. A video started of Jaimie dragging Ember through the hall and into his room.

A few more taps and the video changed, showing them getting into a truck and driving off. The time stamp said it had only been ten minutes ago.

"We should have known he'd be involved."

"Yes." Dak agreed.

"They're not that far ahead." He might catch up to them if only he knew where it was they were going. He'd waste time if he just started driving now. But the kids groaning in pain on his living room floor would have the answers he needed.

Roen, Cole, and Hendrick had finished gathering them to one side of the room. Some bled from non-fatal wounds. Others needed medical attention that King didn't feel inclined to supply. King stared them all down. They'd made a stupid decision to work for Boyd.

"Do any of you know who I am?"

No one answered.

"What was your job here?"

Still nothing.

"Okay. The guy you work for doesn't give a shit about any of you. You're weak, dispensable foot soldiers, which is how the five of us bested the twenty of you. I want answers. Now. And you'll all get to live another day."

A shaking hand lifted above all the heads. "We were told to kill anyone except the girl and to keep everyone distracted from her." The attack in numbers made sense. But did Boyd believe all it took to kill him was high volume?

"Where did he take the girl?"

"Shut up." A kid kicked his foot out into the back of the one giving him answers. "You know what the boss will do if he finds out you talked."

"But what am I going to do if you don't?" King loomed over the group, letting his full monster out. Most of them shrank back, others flinched while they shook with the effort to stay still. "If any of you have even half a cell in your brain, you will realize that I'm much more dangerous than *the boss*. You'll tell me everything, then you will turn your nose back around and keep it cleaner than your mother's ass."

"There's an old lab in the university's basement." The kid had tears running down his cheeks as he rushed to get his words out faster. "That's where he said to take her if any of us found her and got her out."

"If I see any of you caught up in this shit again, I'll kill you on the spot. This world isn't worth your lives." One chance is all King would give any of them.

"He's just bluffing, to scare us." The kid in the back leveraged himself against the wall to stand up. King didn't have time for this shit. He pulled a knife and, in the same motion, launched it across the room. It lodged in his shoulder, pinning him to the wall.

"I can smell the fear in the piss in your pants. I don't bluff."

"Roen and Cole, you take care of these guys." Dak moved in beside him. The faces on the floor blanched. "Hendrick, you're with us."

Ignoring their cuts and gashes, they restocked their weapons and left. King was getting his girl back.

NONE of this should surprise her after all she's seen and learned. Despite finding out about Jaimie's past (change if omitted), it made sense he'd be involved with Dr. Alexander. No, that wasn't right. King had said he'd faked his name and credentials. He still wore his glasses and suit from teaching the summer classes that day. He'd tried to get her to take his summer program.

"Miss Bellamy. I'm happy to see you back at school." Lewis Boyd leaned against the dusty lab bench.

Ember tried for the same icy glare King used.

"I'd hoped King would have gotten lazy over the years, less meticulous. I've been wanting to take that man out for years." Boyd almost vibrated with excitement over King's death. "But when I heard Zax's assassins didn't return, I took a different approach."

"We sent twenty of them in there. There's no way they made it out alive." Jaimie stalked toward Ember. Her stomach revolted. She'd let him touch her. Had willingly kissed him. And he was just as sick and twisted as her instincts tried to tell her. Ember hadn't listened. Brushing herself aside as being silly.

"Don't be so sure. How many of that twenty had the gumption to kill? Do you even have it?" Boyd tilted his head and removed his glasses. Slow eyes assessed Jaimie.

"Of course I do." Jaimie sneered over his shoulder.

"Hmm. We'll see." Boyd pushed off the table. "Will he come for you, Miss Bellamy?"

Ember's throat dried. She didn't want to draw ire from either of them. King had told her he wasn't letting her go. But if he didn't make it out of there, would Dak come? Or one of the others? With her hands and feet tied together in front of her, she couldn't move. She had no weapons, shitty clothes, and no shoes. And she blamed King for that. And he'd get an earful when this was over. Ember kept her lips tight together and took in as many details as possible. The layout of the old lab. The students and ones that looked nothing like students circling the room and coming in and out.

"If he was still alive, he would. She was hiding without a scratch on her. He didn't hurt her." Jaimie crouched in front of her as he gave his assessment.

"The king of mercenaries with a soft heart. Sickening." Boyd removed his jacket and glasses, tossing them over a different lab table. Heavy dust stirred and settled.

"I get to keep her. I got the prize." Jaimie reached out to touch her face and Ember flinched. She didn't wanted to show any sign of emotion, but his touch made her stomach revolt.

"But you didn't kill King." Boyd tilted his head, a half smile lifted his cheek.

Jaimie froze and looked up at Boyd, who now stood beside them.

"Doesn't matter. None of the others even knew there was a prize. Her. I organized it. I keep her."

"I'll make you a deal, boy." Jaimie thought he had more pull than he did, but Boyd's tone whipped back that notion. "If you kill King when he comes in here to get her, you get to keep her."

"And if he doesn't come at all because he's already dead?" Jaimie stood and squared off with the other man.

"I'll consider it."

Jaimie narrowed his eyes, unpleased with Boyd's answer. The prick thought the man owed him for something. The privileged man always got what he wanted.

Ember's lungs hurt from keeping her cries inside. She was so mad at King for leaving her helpless--mad at herself for the same reason. All she wanted was to go home. But where was that? It wasn't with her father. With King? What would it be like to be his queen?

19

———————

A stormy rage clouded around King. Sure footsteps carried him forward until Dak stopped him. He'd nearly taken off his friend's arm.

"Think, King."

He was. He was thinking of Ember. Thinking of barging in, killing anyone in his way, and walking out with Ember in his arms.

But they had to deal with the security first. Not only Boyd's security, but the university's as well. But anytime they stepped in front of a campus security guard, the guard just spun on his heels and carried on in the other direction as if they hadn't seen them. Seemed Boyd had struck a deal with campus security and they must think King, Dak, and Hendrick were part of Boyd's crew.

With the direction of the lab memorized, the three of them spread out. Campus security had thinned and almost vanished after spotting them the first few times. Boyd's deals only made it easy for them.

King kept to the shadows along the concrete buildings. The first kid watched all the wrong places, searching open areas rather than the dark corners near him. Silent and effortless, King pulled him back and knocked him out with a distinct hit to the head.

No sounds echoed from anywhere around him. Dak and Hendrick weren't having any trouble either.

King took care of three more student guards by the time he met Dak and Hendrick at the entrance to the basement. He had to control himself. The urge to barge in, kill them all, and damn the consequences was stronger than he'd ever felt it before. His control never diminished. Why now?

Ember. It was all for Ember.

"You understand the risks?" Dak whispered low beside him.

He nodded. He understood there were only three of them and an unknown number in the lab and that by going in, they risked someone hurting or killing Ember out of spite. King understood all too well that he could lose her.

"Let's go." Dak descended the basement stairs first, surprising a kid at the bottom. Before he could make a sound, Dak dealt with him, then passed him up for King and Hendrick to leave on the stairs. They found two more in the hall, and they weren't as quiet.

"Hey!"

Dak rushed him as another came around the corner. King launched himself, knocking him out in the middle of his warning. He doubted Boyd gave them a clear picture of what they were getting into. But inside that lab, King wouldn't be able to hold back.

King reached for the door, but Dak stopped him.

"Us first. Hendrick, you take left. I'll take right. King, you get to Ember."

King took a breath to steady the killer in him, the

monster that he'd tried to run from with retirement. It embedded in his soul. He'd been foolish to hide from it.

Dak nodded his countdown, then opened the door. They rushed in while darkness engulfed King, slowing each step he took with careful calculation. Dak took out two and Hendrick dealt with another.

A face from the past grinned at him from the centre of the room. He raised his hand, and the attacks stopped. From his guys, but not Dak and Hendrick. They each took down two more, advancing themselves further into the room before stopping.

Cold ice and fiery rage warred as King looked around. Behind Boyd stood Jaimie with a fist in Ember's hair. They'd bound her with rope and she sat on the floor. He needed the cold to deal with Boyd and Jaimie, but the heat pushed back.

"How did I never see it before?" Lewis tilted his head, studying King's face. "King's messenger was the king of mercenaries all along. Very clever."

"And the face of the lowest mercenary never changed."

"Ouch. It hurts." Boyd's deadpan voice didn't echo in the room. He quirked his brow. "Yet here we are. I've got your girl. And wasn't that a surprise to find her unharmed? Your girl." He whistled.

"Call your lapdog off of her and cut her loose." King didn't need to make threats. The other man knew all too well what King would do.

"No. I set up this contest, although I never expected it to come full circle back to me. It surprised me that more didn't jump at the chance to get rid of you for good. Jaimie convinced me to let him try it his way. A deal is a deal. He's going to kill you to get the prize. Fair is fair."

Jaimie released Ember, and she whimpered as her head

slumped forward. King needed to touch her, but he had two things in his way.

Boyd knew King could kill Jaimie with a single finger. He leaned around Jaimie and raised a brown at Boyd.

Boyd shrugged. "He insisted."

Jaimie snarled and attacked, coming in low. King shot up with a knee, snapping his head back. King moved in quick. He grabbed an arm and twisted until he had Jaimie's back to his chest. Feeling none too charitable with the kid who'd touched Ember, King pulled a knife from its sheath at his back and brought it up to Jaimie's throat.

"Bad life choices." He moved the knife from one side to the other. Blood poured and Ember screeched, the sound piercing King's heart. But there was nothing to be done about it. He couldn't hide this from her. This would be the last time she saw this kind of violence. But she needed to see what he was, what he did. Then none of this would touch her again.

Dak and Hendrick had inched around the room to take care of Boyd's thugs that hung in the shadows. His attention hadn't left King.

Boyd pulled Ember's head back with an identical grip in her hair as Jaimie. He smirked while dragging a knife from his back. Ember went wild on the floor, trying to pull her head away and thrashing her bound body against the concrete floor. King's blood pumped as wildly as she did.

"No matter what you do, you aren't walking out of this lab alive." King glared at Boyd, imagining the ways to make his death quick, but extremely painful.

"You've gotten lazy, King. Haven't you noticed that you're surrounded?"

"All your guys are dead." Dak stepped from the shadows on the left. Panic filled Boyd's eyes. He pulled Ember's head back further, and she screamed. King saw the blade inch closer. They didn't have enough time to get to her.

EMBER REFUSED to go out like this. The rope burned her skin the more she struggled, but she wouldn't let him kill her without a fight. King was too far away, and that knife was too close. Boyd's nothing-to-lose grip tightened and pulled, exposing her neck. She'd just witnessed what it looked like to have your throat slit. King had slit Jaimie's throat with ease. She didn't want to die like that, or that fast. She'd watched death leach into his eyes.

His grip held firm, but she didn't let it stop her from thrashing, trying to move away from him. She bounced to twist her feet and hands to the side. Her ass hurt, but not as much as the rest of her would in only seconds. Burning encased her scalp, but she pulled harder against him.

King roared as the knife drew closer while Boyd struggled to keep her in place. She'd twisted herself onto her side and brought her feet up behind him. It wasn't enough to keep her neck away from him, but he stumbled.

King and Dak raced forward. The grip in her hair vanished, and Ember collapsed to the floor. Pain burned in her upper arm, and warmth trickled down.

Tilting her head, her cheek resting against the cold floor. King and Dak had Boyd held firm between them.

"This is going to hurt." Darkness coated King's voice.

Dak stood behind him and inched a knife into his back. King slid one in the front. Both angled upward. They drew them out and Boyd gurgled. They did it again in three different places. Blood pooled in his mouth.

The sight would haunt her, but she couldn't look away

from King's face as he tortured him. King pulled his knife free and stepped back. Her vision blurred, but her eyes remained wide as King struck across his throat.

"Ember?" Her name was muffled in her ears. A heavy hand squeezed her shoulder.

"There you go, sweetheart. All free." Dak crooned low. The pressure released around her wrists and ankles. Painful sensations surged into her limbs, but she blocked it out.

King sat her up on the floor. She didn't blink through his blurry image in front of her. She should fear him after what she saw him do. But she felt nothing.

Someone wrapped something tight around her arm. The burning had ebbed.

"We need to get out of here." A third voice spoke behind her. Her ears rang, and a haze encased her. She wasn't asleep, yet it felt like a dream.

King lifted her into the air. Ember closed her eyes and leaned her head against his shoulder, unable to process anything she saw or heard. She caved and let it happen, but at least she knew she was safe with King.

EMBER WOULDN'T ANSWER HIM. She breathed steadily and the only injuries seemed to be the gash of her arm from Boyd's knife and the raw, angry skin on her wrists and ankles. He settled her against his chest. Before she sank her weight against him, her wide pupils hadn't looked at him, but through him. Her skin paled and chilled.

Was her reaction from being taken by Jaimie and Boyd, or from watching King kill with merciless, cold blood?

"She's in shock. We can't take her back to my place."

Even if Roen and Cole had gotten rid of the leftovers by now, they wouldn't have the bodies or carnage disposed.

"We'll go to my place." Dak walked in front of King, his gaze ever watchful to make sure they didn't run into any trouble while walking through campus to their vehicles.

Ember didn't move as King placed her in the back seat. Her eyes opened, and she tilted her head to look out the window, but King doubted she saw much. Dak and Hendrick slid in the front. King held Ember on his lap. He needed to feel her, feel her heart beating in her chest. Hear her soft breathing below his chin.

"Ember. Talk to me." King whispered against her hair. Her breathing didn't hitch, and she stayed utterly still against him.

Dak pulled up outside his place and opened the back door for King to get out. He handed Ember to Dak, then took her back once he was clear of the vehicle. They walked through to the back of Dak's security business to his private elevator. They rode to the top floor and Dak unlocked one of the two apartments.

The place was immaculate and cold. Nothing personal and all in grey. King carried Ember into the single bedroom. Laying her down, he tried talking to her again.

"Ember, pretty girl. I need you to talk to me."

She curled onto her side and tucked her hands under her chin. Dak came in with a first aid kit in his hand.

"The cut on her arm is deep and still bleeding." The scrap fabric they'd wrapped around had soaked through and fresh blood continued to bloom.

It had to be stitched. He hated doing that while she wasn't lucid. But King nodded. They needed to do it now.

"Ember. You have a cut on your arm. Dak has to give you stitches."

She shivered. It was the only reaction they got saying she'd heard him.

"I'm not leaving you. I've got you." King slid his hands into hers in front of her and she squeezed. Dak climbed onto the bed behind her and peeled back the fabric.

King watched Ember's face, her eyes, her lips. Any sign that she was aware of what was going on.

Dak cleaned the wound and used the numbing cream on her skin. "Sorry, sweetheart." He inserted the threaded needle and pulled it through.

King's worry increased the longer Ember lay still. Unmoving with no emotions. No tears, no sign of pain.

Dak finished the ten stitches needed and packed up the first aid kit. "You should get her cleaned up. Use one of my shirts for her for clean clothes. I'll get Cole to pick some up for her after I check in with them."

"I'm going to get you in the shower now." King tried to lift her up, but her voice breaking free stopped him.

"No." She swallowed as if the single sound hurt.

King wanted to force the issue, but she seemed like she could snap in two at any moment. He let her fall back onto the bed and tucked the blanket up over her. Climbing into bed behind her, he wrapped his arms around her.

His. And he'd failed her. She'd spoken, but she didn't sound like herself. A shell. Not the brave, spiteful woman who'd slapped him or poured coffee on him.

King held her, whispering soft nonsense until her breathing slowed. He wouldn't put her in danger by being in this life, but he wasn't letting her go. King shuddered as he realized this decision wasn't his to make.

20

———

The haze had dispersed the moment they'd left the basement lab, but Ember still didn't react to King or the others. This state of shock suited her fine as she processed everything that happened, everything that she'd seen. She'd slept in King's arms, needing his warmth down to her bones. But when she'd woken, King insisted she shower and eat.

Ember had moved through the motions with him. Showering, dressing in new clothes she didn't recognize. They were pretty. A soft purple sweater and dark jeans, among many other pieces. She didn't know where they'd come from, but she didn't care. She'd looked at them with the same bland expression she'd adopted since she watched King kill Boyd.

Eating took too much energy, but she managed. She caught the worried looks King and Dak exchanged over the past few days. Ember was fine, but she was sorting through her own thoughts, emotions. Assessing herself, her life, her relationship with King.

In the evenings, after King put her to bed, she'd slip from

the sheets and listen at the door. He should have caught her. King and Dak had talked of what police found at the university. Many of the student recruits of Boyd gave up everything. Some dug themselves further.

King's face was no longer a secret. There was a large target on his back and a red dot on his forehead. And where would that leave Ember? They never answered that question, no matter how many times they'd asked it of each other.

Roen and Cole had cleaned up King's house, but King still didn't want to return. It wouldn't only be other mercenaries and criminals after him, but authorities, too.

It was time for her to speak up, to decide for her life. She'd despised herself for being helpless in that position. She didn't have her old life to return to and she never could again. Not without wondering about the ulterior motives of anyone who smiled her way.

King and Dak worked together in the kitchen. It was odd, seeing such domesticity after witnessing how cruelly they'd killed. The dark and the savage.

"What's my role?"

Both men whirled around, wide eyes pinning her in place as if she was a ghost. She'd almost felt like one the way she'd been floating for days.

King dropped the pan with a clang against the stove top and rushed toward her. He gripped her around the waist and lifted her, carrying her to the counter. Plopping her on top, he touched his nose to hers.

"You're okay?" His voice scratched as his hands roamed her shoulders, arms, and sides. Seeing his worry break him snapped her out of her self-imposed shock.

"Yes, I'm fine." She tried to soothe him with her hands through his hair and over his shoulders.

"Thank God." He cupped her face and kissed her. Soft, smooth, but with no less hardness than was King.

"What's my role?" She'd decided and her choice depended on King's answer. Ember loved him. With more than she had. But she almost died because of her ignorance and inability to protect herself. King came for her. But he'd been too far away when it mattered. She'd had nightmares of what would have happened if she hadn't struggled with all her might.

"What do you mean?" His dark eyes that were once terrifying, searched hers.

"What do I do? If I stay with you. Where's my outfit?" She brought their conversation back to before the attack.

"Outfit?" His harsh frown shoved his head back.

"The black fatigues covered in weapons. What am I now?" He wouldn't tuck Ember away.

"Mine, Ember. You're mine." The possessive tone sent a delicious shiver to her core, but she pushed it aside. This was too important.

"Then what's my role?" If he's a king, what did that make her?

King straightened, a gentle coolness shrouding his eyes. "You don't have one."

That hurt. Her heart cracked and her skin stung. She reared her feet up from beside him and shoved at his hips to put distance between them. Dak moved around behind her, picking up where they'd left off in the kitchen. But she had no more embarrassment in front of him. He needed to hear this, too.

"I was helpless. I wasn't strong enough. I had nothing to defend myself. No shoes to run in. No knife hidden beneath my clothes. I was dragged away by my ankles!" She screamed and shoved herself off the counter. "What am I if I stay?" Ember wouldn't accept anything less.

"Mine." King growled. He stepped forward and slid his hand to the back of her neck. "There is no *if*. I'm keeping you."

"I have to be more than just yours. No one will drag me away or use me as a pawn again. If I'm yours, then people should fear me, too."

"Fuck, no. You will never get your hands dirty." And King didn't say things he didn't mean. He wanted her, but he wanted her tucked away and hidden. People would be coming after him now. And when they found out about her, they'd come after her. Well tucked away with no defenses wasn't safe and it wasn't the life she wanted. King and this experience had spoiled her view of the world. But if he wouldn't teach her and make her feared, she'd find some other way to do it.

"Then I don't belong here."

KING REACHED FOR HER, but Dak grabbed his arm.

"Let. Me. Go." The threat didn't affect him. He squeezed tighter and pulled him back.

"She's right."

Ember stiffened at Dak's words before she walked out the door.

"Think about it, King. How is hidden and helpless safe?"

Having her back, lucid in front of him, only for her to walk out, was like a severe case of whiplash. His lungs seized. Watching him in his element had put her in a state of shock for days. He'd been so worried he'd lost her completely. How the hell did she expect to fight beside him? Fuck that. No. She was going to be kept safe.

But she wouldn't be safe away from him.

King ran his hands over his face and threw his hair. Dak let him go.

"This has forced you out of retirement. How do you feel about that?" Dak leaned back against his small kitchen island.

"You want to talk about this now? My feelings toward coming out of retirement?" King didn't give a fuck about his retirement anymore. He only wanted Ember. Working or not, he was no longer in hiding. But he didn't care what he did with the rest of his life. As long as he had Ember there. She wouldn't be if she got herself killed while on a job or defending herself. No. He didn't want any of it touching her. She was the only bright thing in his life. The only thing that made his heart beat since his parents died. He loved her.

"Yeah, I want to talk about this now? You getting back in? Accepting jobs?"

"I don't fucking know." He growled while looking at the closed door, hoping she'd come back in. Where was she going to go? She wouldn't return to her father. "I have to go after her. She shouldn't be alone." King took one step and Dak stopped him again.

"Already taken care of."

"How?"

"I sent a message to Roen to follow her before she even left."

King sighed and turned to Dak. "What is it you're trying to get at?" Might as well get this conversation over so he could go after his girl. And keep her away from her father.

"I've built more than just a security firm here. The guys I hire don't keep their jobs if they can't best me in a fight at least once. And they come into this knowing we won't always be on the legal side of things."

"You want me to come work for you?" The idea didn't sit right with him. Not because he'd have to answer to Dak, but the two have them had never worked that way.

"No. I want to be partners like we always were."

"We never stopped being partners." King looked at his longest friend. His only friend. King had left more than the darkness behind when he'd retired.

"Then listen to me now. Ember isn't safe if she's defenseless."

Train her. Dak thought he needed to train her. But what other choice did he have? Lose her or make sure she was even better than him. Dak said none of his guys stayed if they couldn't best him at least once. Would Ember balk if he pushed her that hard?

Would he ever forgive himself if something happened to her because he kept her hidden and defenseless? No.

King nodded at Dak. "You're right."

"So, are you in?"

In. Was he ready to embrace what was inside him? "Yeah. I'm in."

Dak threw his arms wide and lowered his chin. "Then, I'd like to welcome you to *King's Mercenaries*."

EMBER HAD WITHDRAWN from the university, sighting unsafe conditions. She hadn't been the only one after media blasted Boyd's face as Murray Alexander, University Professor, found dead in the old chemistry lab alongside several students. The university would suffer from this, and maybe never recover. But that wasn't Ember's problem and not the reason she left.

Visiting her father had been a terrible idea. Gear had returned him home while she'd still been in her hazy days at Dak's. One awkward dinner where he'd tried to apologize and failed miserably. Nothing fixed the fact he sent her into danger rather than finding someone to hide her and keep her safe, telling Ember everything from the beginning. When he'd tried to put his foot down over King, saying he forbade her to see him again, Ember walked out. He'd lost the right to weigh in on her choices.

She'd walked out of Dak's building almost two weeks ago to find Roen waiting for her on the sidewalk. He'd said Dak had a vacant apartment in his building, then escorted her back inside to get her settled in. With nowhere else to go, she'd accepted.

Dak had been by to see her, ensuring her King didn't know where she was and that she was free to stay as long as she needed.

She'd signed up for self-defense classes and shooting lessons. It seemed like the most logical place to start. She was lonely, but there was nothing to do about it. It was King she wanted. King she missed. King she loved. But she refused to stand behind him rather than beside him.

Ember shut her apartment door, locking it behind her. Dak had made it clear that if he ever found it unlocked, she wouldn't like the consequences. Not that he clarified those consequences. Tossing her keys on the table, Ember leaned forward. She'd have a bruise or two from class today. They'd sparred for most of it. Ember welcomed the sore muscles. She was learning. Her body was learning.

She straightened. Something wasn't right. But she didn't realize that in time. A large hand clamped over her mouth and an arm bound around hers, pinning them to her sides. He slammed her back against his chest. Her heart raced and her breathing was shallow behind the hand. How the hell had someone gotten past Dak's security? This building was locked up tight.

He dragged her to the centre of her apartment. This couldn't be happening again. Give a girl some time to recover.

Warmth brushed over her ear.

"First lesson." King. Now that she heard his low tone, she recognized his scent, his arms, the curves in his chest, and the height of him behind her. "Pay attention to the minor details. I moved three things when I came in here. Find them." His hand moved from her mouth to her throat, and King moved in a slow circle. She ran her eyes over the moving picture of her open apartment. Everything looked the same. Ember tried harder. It took two turns for her to notice the first one.

"My purse. It's in front of the lamp instead of beside it."

"That was the easy one. What else?"

Ember tried to focus. Her adrenaline still spiked from when he'd grabbed her. But something settled in her chest with his voice, his hands. A tight ball of tension stretched itself out inside her.

"You can't get distracted." He squeezed her throat.

She huffed and forced her eyes to scan as he continued to circle, never pausing to give her a hint.

"The carpet. Is it crooked?" It was slightly out of place. She might be imagining it, or she could have kicked it herself.

"Did I do it?" His tone gave no clue as to the correct answer.

Damn it. She wasn't sure. "Yes."

"Good guess. One more." He loosened his grip around her arms so she could slide them free.

"The calendar. It's turned back to last month." It often took her two weeks to change the month on a calendar. If she hadn't done it that morning, Ember wouldn't have thought anything of it.

"You got it, pretty girl." His praise warmed her. King turned her around, his hand still curving her throat, moving to her nape. "You were right. I don't like it. I don't want you part of this world, but you aren't safe. And that's true whether you're with me or not. You're going to hate me. You're going to curse me. I won't take it easy on you. Not if I'm going to protect you. I have to know you can get out of any situation."

"What are you saying?" Ember looked up at him. His eyes filled with fierce intensity.

"I'll train you. This world will fear you." King slid his hand from her neck down her back. His body lowered in front of her. Reaching into his pocket, he pulled something out, hiding it inside a fist. His knees hit the floor. Ember stood, shocked. King took her hands from his shoulders and opened his fist. He slid something onto her left hand.

"I love you, Ember. My fire. My queen."

"You... You love me?" His possessiveness hadn't left her wondering that he cared. But love?

King nodded. "Never doubt it."

Ember looked down at her hand. He'd slid a gold band on her right finger. Small amber stones encircled a round diamond.

"Do you have something to say to me, little girl?" He gripped her chin, tilting her head down.

"I love you, too."

"Good girl. I told you I wasn't letting you go." King

leaned forward and stood, his shoulder pushing against her hips. Ember ended upside down over his shoulder. "This better be the last time you get kidnapped, little girl. You won't like the consequences otherwise." King left her apartment, slamming the door behind him.

As soon as she'd entered the shadows, she'd never been able to find her way out. The world hadn't been what she'd thought. And there was only one place where she belonged. With him. He was her king.

Join my newsletter to receive special content, the most up to date information on releases, and special promotions.
https://bit.ly/sarahurq

Also, visit my website at...
http://www.authorsarahurquhart.com
... to see my full book list.

Watch for Dak's story in **Shades of Savage, King's Mercenaries Book Two** coming out Fall 2022.

www.ingramcontent.com/pod-product-compliance
Lightning Source LLC
Chambersburg PA
CBHW051222210726

48290CB00003B/749